Echoes

Echoes

Ashley Vogel

Copyright © 2009 by Ashley Vogel.

ISBN: Softcover 978-1-4415-8745-9

All rights reserved. No part of this book may be reproduced or transmitted in any form or by any means, electronic or mechanical, including photocopying, recording, or by any information storage and retrieval system, without permission in writing from the copyright owner.

This is a work of fiction. Names, characters, places and incidents either are the product of the author's imagination or are used fictitiously, and any resemblance to any actual persons, living or dead, events, or locales is entirely coincidental.

This book was printed in the United States of America.

To order additional copies of this book, contact:
Xlibris Corporation
1-888-795-4274
www.Xlibris.com
Orders@Xlibris.com

To my brother and best friend Brian, with out his faith and constant support my dream would never have become reality.

To Mom and Dad, for never going crazy about all the balls of paper and notebooks laying around the house.

To Chad, who spent many nights going to bed alone while I forged ahead and never complained.

And last, but not least:

To Tony and Joe, my partners-in-crime, my rocks, and the most wonderful friends I could ever ask for.

Thank you all for keeping me sane during this process.

"We thought the North Koreans would back off once they saw the American Uniforms."

Phil Day, Task Force Smith

"My God, maybe there's a real war going on!"
Unknown Soldier (upon seeing a South Korean wounded)

PROLOGUE

TO BE PERFECTLY clear, Alden's Hollow and New Alden are the same place. How do I explain this? Alden's Hollow was originally an Irish settlement based on iron ore mining. The main settlement was pretty well preserved and the locals call that section Old Town. New Alden was tacked on later when all the conglomerates had moved in; Wal-Mart, Starbucks, and alike. It also turned out to be Mom's hometown. Grandma and Grandpa Kelly had passed on long before I was born, which spurred Mom's move to Oakdale, where she managed a very nice hotel.

Landon Hart, mom's new beau, is a contractor in New Alden. The most successful as Mom had bothered to point out to me several times leading up to their engagement. Although I hated the idea of leaving Oakdale and all my old friends there, for the first time in my life I'd seen Mom happy.

Mom met Landon through a dating website. Though they were several hours apart, Mom and Landon visited every weekend. Sometimes Landon would come to Oakdale, other times Mom would go to Alden's Hollow. They'd been dating nearly a year when I first met Aiden, who's a Junior like me, thinks he's God's gift to women and the all-star of Alden Senior High, and Sam his twelve year old, very smart but incredibly shy little brother. Sam and I took to each other very well, Aiden on the other hand repelled Mom and I as much as he could. Throwing tantrums and "mixing up" things.

For instance that first Christmas together. Landon put a bug in my ear about a video game that Sam had been bouncing off the wall about, and concert tickets that Aiden had been begging for. I worked part time at a restaurant as a waitress but managed to buy what I hoped would be the perfect Christmas gifts for the new men in our lives. Sam, unsurprisingly, nearly knocked me over when he opened his video game and Aiden even managed to look taken back by the tickets. Sam had been brilliant and got me a Build-a-Bear that I immediately fell in love with. Aiden however chanced it on perfume, which he insisted that I put on right away. It wasn't until later on that night that I recognized the scent, one I was particularly allergic to in a different bottle. While Aiden insisted that there had to be some mix up, I spent a good chunk of my Christmas day lying on the couch scratching at my newly formed hives. It wasn't until Aiden presented me with a pair of flowery oven mitts to "keep me from scratching" that I was positive there'd been no mix up. That had been during our Freshmen year of course, I hoped that Aiden would grow up a bit. Much to no avail.

So two years later, two weeks shy of my Junior year, and only a week shy of the wedding, I foolishly held out hope that Aiden would help me adjust to me new life in Alden's Hollow. Mom and Landon had bought a new house to bring us together as a family, and we hadn't been in the house twenty minutes when Aiden threw his first tantrum. Mom and Landon announced that I'd be getting the room at the top of the stairs. The second biggest and the only other room, other than the Master Suite, that had a bathroom attached. Being the oldest, Aiden who was older than me by four months, naturally thought he deserved the room. Landon promptly fired back that he knew how Sam and Aiden kept a bathroom and being the only girl, I would need the space. Aiden looked like he wanted to keep fighting for it but a sharp look from Landon sent him stomping off to the moving truck to find his boxes.

Outside I met Jeff, and Andy. Friends of Landon's who he had enlisted to do the heavy lifting. Sam and I helped where we could placing boxes in the rooms marked on flaps. Aiden sought only his boxes choosing to isolate himself for the day. Not that I minded truth be told.

The hours passed and it was nearly eight thirty by the time I got around to unpacking my room. I looked at the new four-poster bed that Landon had gotten me as a "welcome to the family" gift. A bed fit for a princess as he had told me. While I was uncomfortable with the idea of being a princess, it was insanely comfortable and a big step up from my old twin bed.

At any rate that was the one part of my room that was sorted out, bed made and all. The other furniture, a desk, a bookcase, and a large arm chair were barely visible under the boxes and bubble wrap. Standing in the center of my room, hands planted firmly on my hips, I sighed wondering where to start.

"That's where it lives." I heard Aiden refer to me, I turned to see him standing in front of my door with a very cute friend.

"Yeah, the bars are on back order, but its okay they installed an invisible fence so I won't get loose for now." I glared at him, his friend chuckled a bit.

"How do I get visitation rights?" he grinned at me, I smiled back at him feeling a little embarrassed.

"Don't even think about it man." Aiden threatened.

"I'm Jerard." his friend ignored him.

"Claire."

"Don't mind Aiden. He just feels threatened by you." Jerard jerked his head at Aiden.

"I ignore him, he's easier to tolerate that way." I nodded subconsciously wondering what my hair looked like.

"My room is down here." Aiden told Jerard pointedly.

"Nice to meet you, Claire. I'm sure I'll see you again." Jerard humored Aiden, I smiled at Jerard and nodded as they left.

It took me a moment to refocus on unpacking. As much as I would have liked to keep Jerard's handsome face in my mind for hours, it wasn't hard to be distracted as I sifted through boxes of my life in Oakdale. The soccer trophies, and photos of old friends, Oakdale High School apparel, all things to make me more homesick then I'd ever been in my life. Eventually boxes were broken down and piled neatly near the door as I finished with them. At the bottom of one of the last few boxes I unpacked I found a very beautiful picture frame, but I was sad to see that the glass had been cracked in the move. I stared at the photo underneath the cracks that looked so like a spider web.

"You look deep in thought." Jerard was leaning against the door frame. The hand that had been hovering over the photo slipped catching one of the shards.

"Damn." I muttered as a few drops of deep red blood bubbled on the tip of my middle finger.

"What happened?" Jerard entered the room, waiving the lack of invitation.

"Cut my finger, the glass broke in the move." I set the frame on my bed and retreated into the bathroom to wash the blood away. Jerard apologized a few times while I clotted the blood with a bit of toilet paper.

"It's okay. It's not that big of a deal, I promise." I laughed as he followed me back into my bedroom. Jerard picked up the photo on the bed.

"Is this your dad?" He looked at me, "Is that you?"

"Yeah . . ." I hugged my arms to me.

"You look a lot like him, you know?" Jerard went on.

"Yeah, I get that a lot."

"Where's he now?"

"He died."

Jerard looked at me, "I'm sorry, Claire."

"Me too." I felt a hot tear slip out of the corner of one of my eyes. Jerard carefully set the photo back on my bed and pulled me into his arms. I couldn't explain the sudden surge of warmth and familiarity I felt as he hugged me. Any other time I would have been frozen solid at the prospect of a cute boy wanting anything to do with me, but something felt so easy about him, so natural, that I couldn't imagine anyone else comforting in the same way that he was.

"Hey Claire, did one of my boxes get put in here? I can't find my Game Cube . . ." Sam walked into the room. Jerard and I broke apart, reluctantly on my end, and I wiped the tear away.

"Yeah, Sammy, I found it earlier." I went to the desk and retrieved the box that sat there.

"Aiden's going to be mad." Sam jerked his head in the direction of Jerard.

"Aiden's always mad. Don't worry about it 'kay? I'll sort out Aiden." I patted Sam on the shoulder and he nodded before leaving the room. I felt Jerard come up behind me.

"I guess I'll let you finish unpacking."

"Oh, right." I turned to face him. Mentally I was begging him not to go, but being semi sane still, I didn't say it.

"Good night Claire." Jerard cupped my cheek in his hand and his icy blue eyes burned into me for a moment leaving me frozen as he left the room.

My room was in shambles still the next morning. After what had happened with Jerard I just couldn't concentrate anymore. Mostly I laid awake in bed trying not to think of what a disaster everything could be here. Though admittedly it was better to think about that than let my mind stray to Jerard, it was stupid to crush on him. I wasn't the cheerleader type and well Jerard? I was pretty willing to bet that he was.

Downstairs I heard everyone in the kitchen. Mom and Landon were singing along to the radio, and Sam was laughing openly at them. I was reluctant to open my eyes, my mind lingered on the dream I was having. One in which Jerard had gone to war and we'd be writing letters back and forth. It was strange but I had to admit, Jerard looked really handsome in a uniform.

After a moment or two I pulled myself out of bed and headed down stairs. I'd barely touched the stairs when I heard the breaking of glass.

"I *don't* like pancakes! Do you listen to me at all? Or just your precious Claire? I told you Sam . . ." Aiden was making a scene; he came stomping up the stairs, nearly knocking me down them in the process. Mom rushed past me as I entered the kitchen, Landon hot on her heels. At the island, Sam sat stony eyed chewing his pancakes slowly.

"Hey Sammy, it'll be okay." I put my arms around him. Sam stared up at me as if not really seeing me. "It will be. Mom loves you guys, no matter what Aiden thinks."

"I'm sorry about Aiden." Sam gulped looking quite miserable. "He never used to be like this. After Mom left he kinda went haywire."

"Don't apologize for him." I moved to pick up the broken shards of plate. "You two are nothing a like. You're responsibility is to yourself, not him. Remember that. And he can't blame whatever issue's he's having on your Mom. He needs to grow up already."

"But he is my brother. And I'm fine with you and Amelia, but Mom leaving affected us in different ways. Aiden doesn't want a new mom. I do though, I never really had one." Sam mentioned wisely. Poor Sam, so older than his twelve years. I looked at him and nodded.

"I know Sammy, I know."

Mom was going absolutely mad the day of the wedding. I tried to remind her several times that she had, in fact, done this once before, but I think her sisters were making her that way. Making sure she had "Something Old, Something New, Something Borrowed and Something Blue." and their prissy daughters didn't help much. Truth be told I was always the tomboy of the girls in our large Irish family. My Mom was one in seven children, which meant lots of family, lots of fighting and lots of dramatics. My Aunt Christine's daughter, who was a sophomore in college, Carolyn, was barking out orders to everyone in the family until I had enough of it.

"Alright!" I bellowed, "Everyone except Aunt Ellen, Aunt Adele and Aunt Christine, hit the road!" Everyone turned to look at me. "I'm serious! Out! That especially means you Carolyn, it's mom's day she doesn't need everyone making her stressed out." I held the door open and reluctantly my cousins filed out, Carolyn put up a last stitch effort to stay but my mom flat out told her to go, earning her a glare from her older sister. Carolyn was the first grandchild and considered the princess of the family. Aunt Christine hated it when anyone treated her as anything less.

"Well look who got a voice." Aunt Christine sneered as I closed the door. "Who are you to tell anyone what to do?"

"She's my mom." I glared back at her, Aunt Christine and I had never gotten along. She had never approved much of my dad and openly said so.

"And she's my sister. See Amelia, if you'd married a nice Irishmen like me you wouldn't have to worry about such bad genes tainting the family." Aunt Christine stared directly at me.

"If I married and Irishmen like you Christine, I'd have ten children and no career to speak of. Claire is perfect the way she is." Mom fired back at her. Aunt Christine's mouth worked furiously but nothing came out.

"Well, that put me in my place. I'll go find Henry then, since I'm obviously not wanted around here." Aunt Christine shuffled out of the room in search of the oldest Kelly brother. Uncle Henry was walking Mom down the aisle.

"It's about time you stood up to her Amelia." Aunt Adele nodded approvingly.

"Well done." Aunt Ellen agreed.

"Well she thinks she's the matriarch of the family since Mom died. But no one can stand her." Mom fumed.

"Mom, it's not about Aunt Christine today, today is your day. If she wants her dramatics, let her have them. But don't let it ruin today, today's about you and Landon." I said to her.

"You're right honey, you look so pretty, have I told you that?" Mom smiled at me, playing with a loose spiral curl. "So grown up."

"Thanks, Mom, you look great too." I smiled back at her. I vaguely heard Aunt Adele and Ellen sigh contently.

Aiden and I stood in the back of the small Catholic church in Old Town. The very same in which Grandma and Grandpa Kelly had been married in decades before. Landon had just walked down the aisle, Mom and Sam stood behind us, Aiden and I were serving as Best Man and Maid of Honor, unfortunately that meant two things: we were forced to walk down the aisle together, and later I got to make an incredibly horrible speech in front of tons of people. I love mom, but I will get her for this one day. Landon was at the alter, which meant it was our cue to link arms, pretend we liked each other, and stroll casually down the aisle. Easier said then done really, at least on the liking each other end, though we did make it to the alter with out killing each other and that had to be a plus. Sam strolled after us, reluctantly holding a ring bearer's pillow in hand and stood next to Aiden.

The priest asked everyone to rise in honor of the bride, and we all turned to watch Mom saunter down the aisle with Uncle Henry looking happier than I can ever remember seeing her.

I'd like to say that I focused on Mom the entire time, but really she was moving so slow soaking up the attention she rightfully deserved, and you can only stare at the same thing for so long before you get bored. So my eyes strayed to the audience. In the third row a few younger cousins were playing hand held video games, which worked out quite well because they would have been fighting the entire time. In the very last row a relative on Landon's side was talking quietly on a cell phone, that one made me kind of angry. I mean come on, the ceremony wasn't going to be that long, shut the damn thing off. A few rows up from the annoying Hart relative my eyes laid upon Jerard sitting in between an extremely pretty blonde girl and a native looking boy who had to be taller than Jerard was. At that moment Jerard looked towards the front and I could was sworn he winked at me, but of course, I was just being foolish. No way would a boy as cute as Jerard do that to me.

Now don't get me wrong, I'm not completely horrible looking. Back at Oakdale High I'd had a few boyfriends but they were very ordinary looking guys. Not that there's anything wrong with ordinary but Jerard – Jerard looked like a casual rock star. You know, take away all the accessories and stuff the stylists make them wear. I smiled at him surprised that he had managed to put on a three-piece suit, most guys our age couldn't manage khakis.

The ceremony was a short exchange of vows, the lighting of a unity candle and the kiss to seal the deal. Quite simply Landon and Mom had both been married once already and neither of them saw the point to drag it all out with a full Catholic mass and everything. Everyone jumped to their feet and applauded the happy couple as we all made our way to exit the church. Truth be told I was glad the ceremony was over, even though I knew all eyes were on Mom, I was too close to her to be able to pretend that people weren't staring at me too.

Just outside the doors Mom and Landon hugged us all. Their excitement of us all being a family was too much for any of us to really deal with at that point. Aiden, Sam and I mostly nodded and smiled before standing just beyond them in the receiving line.

Aiden, who stood between Mom and I, was content to ignore Sam and I completely as we greeted family members and friends from all over the country. Sam was nice enough to keep a running commentary of who was who in his family, and I of course did the same for him. Neither of us did anything of the sort for Aiden.

I liked twinkle lights, and was content to stare at them as they lined the large white tents Mom and Landon had rented for their reception in Alden City Park. At the round table I was sharing with Jerard, Aiden, his Barbie esque girlfriend Shannon were three of their friends. Shannon's counterpart, Anabel Stephens, was every bit as pretty as Shannon was with strawberry blonde hair and a face full of cute freckles. The other two were boys; Ryan Winters and Key Loonsfoot. Ryan was the typical surfer boy complete with a charming smile and sandy blonde hair. Key on the other hand stood out in the group. He was tall with rust colored skin and long raven hair but just as handsome as the rest of the group.

Aiden, though his anger towards Mom and I had been put on hold, still made it known that he wasn't happy with me invading his group of friends. Every time someone laughed at something I said, Aiden would glare at me, or change the focus to someone or anything else. Jerard, of course, was always good to ignore his friend though, and Shannon too. Something I was sure irritated him even more; his best friend and his girlfriend taking the wicked step sister's side.

Shannon and Ana were huge romantics and among the first to scramble onto the dance floor when all the single girls were called for the bouquet toss. It was only after Mom had told the DJ that I was missing and he personally called me out that I joined them. Though wasn't surprised when it turned into the battle for the bouquet between Shannon and two of Aiden's cousins. Shannon looked sweet, and cute and innocent but she was the one who ended up with the bouquet. Only after I was sure one of them had been elbowed with in an inch of their life. Jerard, Key, Ryan and I watched with great joy when Shannon returned with the disheveled bouquet and started to plan out their wedding with Ana. However the awkward way Landon removed Mom's garter with his teeth sobered me up pretty quickly.

It was around the time that all the couples had gone out for the love bird dance that I needed to get away from the ooey gooey love moments today.

"Wanna go for a walk?" Jerard noticed the horrified look on my face.

"Please." I nodded.

It was a friendly gesture, Jerard had extended a hand out to me to help me up from my chair, but it turned into something much more.

"Miss?" He bowed to her slightly helping her from the chair.

"James, you are so cute." Ona giggled taking his hand. In the background a trumpet crooned the slow intro to a very beautiful ballad. His grin fell away as he held her close to him, one strong hand around her back, the other feather light around her own small hand. Ona leaned her cheek to James' jaw, they swayed to the music completely unaware of the other couples swirling around them.

"Come back to me, James." she whispered to him. James took the smallest of steps back and cupped her face in his hands.

"Nothing could keep me from coming back to you." he looked her dead in the eye. *"I love you Fiona."*

Fiona melted into James again not allowing him to see the tears leaking from her light gray eyes. This was her last night with James. Tomorrow he would be on a plane for Korea and only the good lord himself knew whether or not he'd really return. She didn't want to let go of him. The future was too uncertain, too scary for her to imagine with out James.

As if I'd been sucked back into reality, I was surprised to find myself on the dance floor with Jerard. I looked up at him in question, the same dazed look on his face. As other senses returned to me I heard the laughter of wedding guests enjoying the party, I smelled the night air, and I felt Jerard's around wrapped almost protectively around my waist. I was confused, I wasn't sure how I'd gotten on the dance floor with Jerard. Really, I would have liked to stay there in that moment for the rest of the night, but Aiden had other plans. I think we were both taken by surprise when Aiden wedged us apart. I couldn't do anything but watch as Aiden shoved Jerard off in the other direction. Alone on the dance floor I hugged my arms around me and made my way back to the table.

The night didn't get much better. Not even an hour later Uncle Angus, Aunt Christine's husband, threw a punch at Uncle Liam – the younger Kelly brother after having too much to drink. Though it was only around ten o'clock the party started to disperse. Mom kept her cool, but I knew that the next day she and Aunt Christine would have it out.

Finally, Mom and Landon whisked away to their hotel room in New Alden's nicest hotel. While Aunt Ellen oversaw the clean up, men that Landon had hired in white jump suits to dismantle everything and take it back to the vendors. I was about to go home to play referee to Aiden and Sam when Shannon and Ana caught me. They demanded that I come to their sleep over claiming that after a week of Sam and Aiden they were sure I was in great need of girl time, and truth be told I was, Aiden was enough to drive any girl crazy. Jerard, being the nice guy he was, offered to take me home to get clothes for tomorrow and bring me to Shannon's on the way to his house in New Alden. Shannon and Ana grinned at me in a way that told me I'd have to explain my connection to Jerard later, but agreed to that arrangement.

With old world manners Jerard helped me into his silver Jeep Liberty and maneuvered masterfully around other departing guests. We rode through the dim streets of Old Town, but dim didn't mean that they were lifeless. We passed several houses enjoying barbeques and fireworks, children and adults a like enjoying the last bit of summer. We even had to stop for a twilight game of baseball being played in the street.

"So . . ." Jerard started, "What's the deal with your aunt?"

"Aunt Christine? Big mouth, perma-glare?" I grinned at him.

"Yeah that one." he laughed.

"She's just a pain in the ass. Grandpa and Grandma died ages ago and since then, being the second oldest daughter she thinks she needs to keep everyone together, but everyone just humors her because we'd all have to hear about it if we didn't."

"Shouldn't that be the oldest daughter's job?" He inquired.

"Aunt Ona died when she was eighteen. Pneumonia or something." I replied. "It goes Ona, Henry, Christine, Eleanor, Adele, Amelia and Liam."

"I'm sorry to hear that. She was really young." Jerard turned a corner.

"Yeah, She was going to get married I think too." I tried to think back. No one really talked about Aunt Ona, and when we mentioned her the family quickly changed the subject.

Back at the house Jerard and I walked in on World War III between Aiden and Sam. Aiden had Sam in a half nelson and Sam was doing everything he could to get out of it.

"Aiden stop!" I barked at him. "Don't make me call Mom and Dad tonight!"

"Break it up you guys." Jerard stepped between the two, pulling Aiden off of Sam. Aiden threw Sam down and retreated up to his room. I rushed to help Sam up, but he too pushed me away and stomped up the stairs. A moment later we heard two doors slam respectively. I turned to Jerard.

"I can't go anywhere tonight. These two will kill each other. I bet Sam was defending me." I added after a moment.

"Go hang out with the girls." Jerard said, "I'll come stay with Aiden and keep him busy, okay?"

"You're parents won't mind the short notice?" I thought about it.

"My parents are in Egypt. They won't even know I'm not home." He shook his head.

"How long are they away?"

He shrugged, "I don't know. They call once a week to check on me."

"Sounds lonely." I looked up at him.

"My Aunt Jodi keeps an eye me."

"Well, I'm glad you'll stay here tonight then, I'd hate to think of you being alone." I replied finally. "I'll get my stuff."

Jerard walked me to Shannon's door and waited until Mrs. Snow opened it.

"Hello Jerard, you must be Claire. I'm Haylee Snow, Shannon's mom." Mrs. Snow extended her hand to me.

"Nice to meet you, Mrs. Snow." I shook hands with her.

"Oh please, call me Haylee. We'll take her from here Jerard." Mrs. Snow said politely.

"Have fun." He muttered to me, "Goodnight Haylee."

"Bye Jerard." Haylee and I chorused.

"Come in, dear, come in." Haylee ushered me in to the house. "Shannon! Claire is here!"

Ana and Shannon came in from the kitchen their arms full of junk food.

"Hi Claire!" they came to me.

"Here, let me help you . . ." I caught a bag of twizzlers just as they slipped out of Shannon's grasp.

"Good catch." Ana nodded, as I took a six pack of Pepsi from her too.

"Come on, we're up stairs." Shannon motioned towards the stairs with her head. I shifted the stuff in my arms and followed Shannon up the stairs and into what wasn't surprisingly a very pink room. One wall was covered with full length mirrors with a ballet bar mounted on it. Around the room there was other ballet related products, point shoes, leotards, and famous ballet posters, Swan Lake and The Nutcracker among others.

"You're a ballerina?" I was a little surprised. Shannon followed my gaze to a set of ballet slippers closest to me.

"I dance, I'm not nearly as good to be called a ballerina though." Shannon shook her head. I shrugged, it was still pretty cool.

I chose to watch, rather than participate, in the mock rock show that Shannon and Ana were putting on using hair brushes as microphones. Some mid-nineties Backstreet Boys song blaring through the speakers of her laptop. I sat with my own laptop and a can of Pepsi watching and laughing each time they pulled something goofy.

"Claire, aren't you going to have any fun?" Ana demanded falling onto the bed next to me.

"I am having fun. You two are quality entertainment." I grinned at her. Ana rolled her eyes and resumed dancing.

"Come on, Claire!" Shannon chimed.

"I don't know any Backstreet Boys stuff." I told her, hoping to get out of making an idiot out of myself. "I was a Hanson fan."

With out missing a beat Shannon jumped off her bed, over to the computer. She sifted through her Itunes folder and gave a song a particularly energetic tap. There was a moment pause while the computer switched songs and the room was filled with the opening chords to MMMBop. Shannon, in an over exaggerated way I might add, danced over to me and started singing loudly and off key to the first verse. Defeated I had no choice but to accept hair brush number three from Ana and join in the "fun."

Soon enough energy drained from the pair and Ana and Shannon set out to plan what Shannon called the Annual Snow Back to School Party. I was happy to just take notes. I gathered very quickly that though while they were very much girlie girls, they were very kind and friendly people. They wanted me included in everything they were talking about and were never got annoyed when I asked who or what something was.

Anyway, the party was started when Shannon got into seventh grade. She wanted to have a back to school party but didn't want anyone to feel left out. So after coaxing her parents, her dad a lawyer and her mom the editor of the town newspaper, she convinced them to let her the entire seventh grade class and their parents come. Ever since it's been a tradition as long as Shannon planned it.

Though I'd really hoped it wouldn't come to this, after all the major planning had been done, the topic changed to boys. Shannon gave up more information than was really needed about where she and Aiden had slipped off to during the early part of the wedding. I don't care if Aiden wasn't blood related – I don't care to hear any of the sorted details about his make out skills. Ana, it turned out, had a pretty big crush on a boy named Declan Sullivan. Yet another large Irish family in Alden's Hollow. He was one in five kids and apparently had a heart of gold and a body just as solid. He was on the swim team and she had told me and never missed a meet. Somehow I doubted whether or not he beat a state record was the reason she went. I tried to stay away from it as long as I could by asking more questions about Declan or making jokes about Aiden, but they cornered me about Jerard.

"So spill it girl, what's going on with you two?" Shannon handed me a few twizzlers.

"Nothing, I don't think?" I replied uncertainly, which was the truth. Other than the few odd moments we've shared there really was nothing solid to go on.

"Everyone who believes that raise their hand." Ana looked around at us. Unfortunately I was the only to raise my hand. My two new friends crossed their arms in front of them, expectant smirks splashed across their faces.

"Really!" I laughed, "We danced at the wedding. That's it." Ana and Shannon exchanged looks of disbelief.

"Well Aiden thinks he likes you." Shannon told me.

"I bet he loves that too." I told her

"Well, you know Aiden." Shannon shrugged.

"I don't. He doesn't talk to any of us. Well Mom and me."

"Oh. Well he's just . . . I don't know, threatened by you. You and your mom are changing his world. He got used to it just being him, Landon and Sam after their mom walked out six years ago." Shannon explained.

"So its Mom and my fault that his mom walked out?" I raised a brow.

"Not exactly. He's just doesn't trust easy."

Shannon took me home the next day in her cute little Neon. The car was bright blue and tiny just like her. I didn't know if I was jealous of the car or just the fact that she had one and I didn't but it was still nice.

The house was quiet when we walked in. Knowing Sam and Aiden they were probably still asleep, but we found Sam in the kitchen working his way through a bowl of Lucky Charms and he told us that Jerard and Aiden were still sleeping upstairs.

So Shannon went to find Aiden and I found Jerard in the guest room across the hall. I expected him to be sprawled out in the middle of the bed, but he was curled up to one side his hair falling over his closed eyes. I sat on the bed next to him, and gently brushed the hair out of his eyes before speaking to him quietly.

"Jerard? Are you going to wake up sometime today?" Jerard stirred slowly, his eyes blinking as the mid day sun came through the partially closed blinds. When his blurry eyes focused on me he smiled.

"If I'm dead I must be in heaven, I'm lucky enough to wake up to an angel." I smiled feeling slightly embarrassed.

"Not dead. No angels. Just me and good ole' Alden's Hollow."

"I'll take it." He rolled over onto his back.

"Everyone's still alive, I see."

Jerard stretched, "Yeah, Aiden was pretty easy to keep busy. Sam stayed in his room most of the night."

"Poor Sammy." I sighed. "Aiden's such a jerk to him." Jerard nodded sleepily.

"Well, I'm back to play referee if you want to go home." I ran a hand through my hair.

"I'd rather stay and enjoy the company, if you can stand me." Jerard replied. I tried to think of any universe in which I would actually want him to go anywhere, but never came close to an answer.

Mom and Landon came home around two from their 'mini honeymoon' in New Alden. Jerard, Sam and I were watching a movie in the living room, but Aiden and Shannon hadn't been seen for hours. Landon made his way upstairs to check on them as Mom offered to make us something to snack on. After a little while Sam went upstairs to get his stuff ready for the next day, while Shannon and Aiden were busted in his room and Jerard and I settled for going for a walk to get out of the awkward tension of the two sitting on separate couches in the living room.

MONDAY

MY ALARM CLOCK was a particularly loud crack of thunder around 5 am. After a half an hour of unsuccessful attempts to sleep, I crawled out of my very warm, very comfy bed and into the shower. I didn't really want to be awake, but I enjoyed a long shower. Landon's major stroke of genius was when he installed what appeared to the eye, in my pint sized bathroom, was that he put my very own water heater in a small room behind it. That meant I could take as long of a shower as I wanted and not have to worry about Aiden whining to Mom and Landon that I'd used up all the hot water.

The tiny bit of typical girl in me thought the first day of school outfit was key, even more when the first day was at an entirely new school. I must have sifted through a dozen outfits until finally deciding on my favorite jeans and a fuzzy pink sweater, I put on my usual mild make up and blow dried my hair.

"Claire?" Sam poked his head in my room. "Jer's here, he wants to take you to school."

"He . . . what?" I turned to look at him properly, I had no clue he was coming, but Sam was starting 7th grade this year and officially moving into Alden Jr. High. He couldn't have looked more terrified. "You okay, kiddo?"

"Yeah, um, Claire? Your mom isn't going to embarrass me when she drops me off is she?" Sam looked rather pale.

"Mom's pretty cool about that." I shook my head, but Sam didn't look entirely convinced. "I can ask Jerard if we can drop you off, if that'd make you feel better?"

"Yeah! Thanks Claire!" Sam disappeared into the hall and I finished getting my stuff together.

I put my tan Fleur di lies messenger bag over my shoulder and headed quickly down the stairs. In the kitchen, Mom was trying to convince Jerard to have some pancakes when I appeared in the doorway to the kitchen. I felt an inexplicable calm wash over me when I saw him. Jerard wore slightly baggy jeans and a short sleeved black button up shirt, and his hair was tied back in as much of a ponytail as he could manage. I tilted my head at him mentally noting how good he looked.

"Good morning, Claire." Landon shuffled past me.

"Morning, Landon." I quietly followed him into the kitchen.

"Pancakes honey?" Mom offered.

"I'm okay, thanks mom." I declined watching Aiden devour a huge stack of pancakes at the island for a moment before turning to Jerard. "Is it cool if we drop Sammy off?"

"Yeah, sure." Jerard smiled at me.

"Oh, I can drop him off Jerard." Mom waved him off.

"Um Mom, I love you, but it's the kids first day of junior high, he can't be dropped off by his step mom, no matter how cool you are." I stepped in.

"She's got a point, Amelia." Landon winked at me, he knew exactly what we were up to.

"It's really not a problem, Mrs. Hart." Jerard tacked on. Mom hesitated. "Well if you're sure . . . ?"

"Absolutely."

Jerard, Sam and I pulled up to Alden Jr. High a few minutes later and Sam looked even more terrified then I felt.

"Want us to come in with you?" Jerard offered as the Jeep idled near the curb.

"No, I-I'll be okay. Thanks Claire, thanks Jer." With that Sam ventured off toward the school, the early morning haze blurring the lines of his body.

"He'll be okay." Jerard assured me as we pulled away.

"I know, I'm just a little attached to Sam is all."

"He's a good kid." Jerard agreed, "You look really nice by the way."

"I thought I was going to have to ask Aiden to show me around." I felt my face burn a little, and decided to change the subject.

"He would have," He flashed me a grin. "grudgingly."

Jerard pulled into a parking space in the student lot a few minutes later and I slid out of the Jeep, adjusting my messenger bag in the process. I waited for him staring, terrified, up at the school.

"What's wrong?"

"Nervous." I admitted reluctantly.

"It'll be okay." Jerard's hand found mine. "Ryan, Shannon, Ana and I are all going to help you out." My stomach turned again, but I felt more relaxed as he led the way towards the school.

The florescent lights gleamed up at us from the almost overly waxed floor. So much that I actually put my sun glasses on. Jerard laughed openly at me until he slid is own Oakley's on. Then he took me to the office to get copies of our schedules, Mrs. Prince the secretary, talked at great length about having mom and my aunts and uncles at Alden Senior High. Apparently my uncle Henry was quite the troublemaker. Then he walked with me around the two huge buildings pointing out places and things to me.

My morning was pretty quiet and I was starting to get really sleepy up until gym class. Yes, I was plagued with gym that semester, but at least it got me energized. Mrs. Adams, the girls teacher, gave us the option to change and play Kick Ball with the boys or not. I became my teams secret weapon, not that any of the guys would have ever admitted it. My team captain Josh, who had no problems letting me know that he didn't want the only girl brave enough to play on his team, did give me a pat on the back when I was responsible for a good chunk of the outs on my side of the field.

I waited outside in the hallway after I'd changed back into my normal clothes. I was content to keep to myself, but the cheerleaders a few feet away weren't about to let that happen.

"New girl." The black haired one approached me.

"Claire." I glared at her, it wasn't often that I took an immediate dislike to someone but this girl was one of those people.

"Whatever, if I ever see you with my boyfriend again, you're going to wish you were never born." She declared, I stared at her in shock.

"You're dating Rex?" I was surprised to say the least. Rex was this guy in my English class, he'd showed me the way to my art class. He was a nice guy, but hardly Brad Pitt.

"Rex Darwin? No way, I'm talking about Jerard Lane. Stay away from him." Before I could respond the bell rang and the cheerleader walked away.

I tried to shake off the feeling taking me over. I felt like I was falling over the edge of a cliff. I'd been crushing on Jerard since the day I met him, but not once had he mentioned a girlfriend. I would have been sure that Aiden would have loved to be the one to send my day dreams crashing to the ground but even he hadn't said anything, anything at all. I was almost to Mr. Goetz's math class when I nearly hit someone coming around a corner.

"Watch where you're going, skank." a bleach blond Barbie snapped at me. I eyed the girl, she wore a pink tank top and a white skirt that I was sure was breaking school dress code being as short as it was.

"You're wearing that and I'm the skank?" I raised a brow at her. Her face contorted, "You're new, I'll pretend like I didn't hear that."

"Don't do me any favors." I retorted, anger starting to rise in me.

"It's probably better if I do." she smiled sharply. "You wouldn't want to be an outcast on your first day."

"I am so not in the mood for this right now."

"Ah, Bianca Hammonds, Queen bitch of Alden Senior High." the tone was so harsh that I found it hard to believe those words had come from Jerard. He was standing behind me, eyes narrowed.

"Jerard, have a good summer?" her voice was just as cold.

"The less I saw of you the more I hoped you'd been sent to Alaska. Isn't there a juvenile detention center there?" Jerard's hand rested on my shoulder. Barbie girl stamped her foot in irritation.

"Why don't you run along and torture the chess club or something." With that Jerard steered me away from her.

"You're like a bad penny." I looked up at him.

"I have you on GPS." Jerard winked at me. I laughed uneasily as we walked into Mr. Goetz's room just after the bell. We received reproachful looks from the teacher and sat in the only two empty seats, he took one near the middle of the room, and I took the other in the front row. Fifty mind numbing minutes later the bell rang and I started putting my stuff in my bag.

"You didn't hear a word of what he said did you?" Jerard was waiting in front of my desk. I stood up and glanced at Mr. Goetz.

"Not really, I've never been good at math." I shook my head following him out of the classroom. "Numbers just get jumbled in my head."

"I can help you." he replied, "If you want."

"It'd be like beating your head against a brick wall."

"That's okay. I've been friends with Aiden forever." He smiled at me and I smirked back.

"Heads up!" we heard someone call. We both looked up and a soccer ball was whizzing towards me. Instinctively I trapped it with my chest to the ground. I got my toe under it and brought the ball back up to my hands. Jerard looked at me in surprise.

"Not bad, new girl." a burly looking boy with a shaved head came up to me. "Do you play?"

"Once upon a time." I replied giving the ball back to him, I turned to Jerard, "He is the second person to refer to me as the "new girl." Do you guys really get that few new kids here?" Jerard shrugged.

"You should try out for the girls team, they could use some new blood." the boy went on ignoring Jerard.

"Nah, I did the sports thing, I'm over it." with that I looked at Jerard and walked away.

"Soccer star?" he looked at me.

"Youth soccer. Oakdale had a good league." I shrugged as we neared my locker. "Who was that?"

"Tim Foster, he plays defense I think." Jerard replied.

"At least he can clear a ball. That's comforting, they might have a shot." Jerard smiled as I opened my locker, set my math book on the shelf and grabbed my sack lunch from the bottom. Jerard tried to sum up today's math class on the way to his locker.

By the time we neared the lunchroom I almost understood it. I was, however, decidedly cold towards him. Making no more conversation then was needed. So cold in fact that we walked through the lobby and commons area in complete silence.

The cafeteria was a large rectangular room lined on the right by large glass windows looking out into the courtyard. It was mostly covered in long white tables with blue and yellow plastic chairs seated along the edges. In the central area of the room were circular tables with similar chairs. We'd barely stepped into the room when Ana came bounded up to us. She chattered wildly about something that had happened in the previous hour, I nodded at the appropriate places but I was, more than anything, glad to have some sort of barrier between Jerard and I. I was trying to sort out my feelings. It was irrational to feel hurt, but I felt it, it was stupid to feel like I should have saw this coming, but I felt stupid. Boy did I feel stupid.

"How you doin' girl?" I felt an arm slip around my waist, I looked up in surprise, to find Ryan. I could tell he was totally joking, but Ana and Jerard just stared at him for a moment. We were just about to a table where Shannon and Key were waiting for us, when Shannon stared between us confused. I gave a noncommittal shrug as I sat between her and Ryan. Jerard sat across from me doing his best to look nonchalant.

Despite it all, Shannon launched right into filling us all in on the post summer gossip. I zoned out to the sack lunch Landon had made me, still warm tomato soup and a grilled cheese sandwich. It wasn't until I heard the voice I'd learned to hate during the last hour that I popped back into reality a few minutes later.

"Hi Jer." The cheerleader from hell practically fell into Jerard's lap.

"Hey Persephone." Jerard looked surprised but happy about the situation he'd found himself in.

"Are you eating with us, Seph?" Shannon asked in a tone that plainly stated she hoped she wasn't. "I don't think there's room for you."

"That's okay I'm happy where I am." Persephone replied dreamily. That was all I needed.

"You can have my seat." I stood up gathering my thermos and sandwich. "I wanted to sit outside anyway, it's too nice."

"Claire . . . ?" Jerard started.

"Good, you don't need to be here, new girl." she said in a sickeningly sweet tone that I was sure no one had heard that actual malice in it.

"Hey Claire, want some company?" Key asked. Surprised, I nodded and headed for the double doors heading out into the courtyard. There was stone statue in the middle of the courtyard that we sat at the base of.

"So, are you trying to screw all this up?" Key asked bluntly.

"Screw what up?"

"You and Jer? And what was with you and Ryan? Are you trying to make him jealous?" Key was usually a very happy-go-lucky kind of guy, it surprised me to see such a serious look from him.

"Come on Key, you know Ryan better than that, he was just goofing around. Besides, how could *I* make anyone jealous?" I countered.

"I know Ryan thinks you're hot, and that if Jer doesn't want you he does. I also know that Persephone's scared stiff, why do you think she's all over Jer?" Key motioned as the light breeze caught his hair, to the lunchroom.

"Cause she's a whore and doesn't care who knows it?" I tilted my head at him. Even Key, who was trying to be serious, couldn't hold back a laugh.

"She and everyone else knows that Jer's zeroing in on you and wants to stake claim by intimidating you." Key shook his head even though I could still see his smile.

"Jerard is *hers*. If he wants me – than he needs to break up with her." I jerked my head towards the glass windows.

"What? Who told you that?" Key's eyebrows arched in curiosity.

"She did."

"And you believed her?" he laughed.

"What other option did I have?" I glared at him,

"Well, take her on then, Shan can't keep a secret. So go after him, he's not dating anyone. We'd know, cause Ryan would be all over you. And him." Key urged me.

The bell rang and Key and I dumped our garbage before catching up with Jerard, Shannon and the rest. Key nudged me, and purposely falling out of balance I knocked into Jerard.

"Oh sorry, Jerard." I apologized touching his shoulder where I'd fallen into him.

"No problem." Jerard looked at me strangely.

"Sorry about the misunderstanding too." I went on glancing at Key.

"Misunderstanding?"

"Yeah, I didn't know you were taken. I wouldn't have been all flirty at the wedding." I went on.

"Taken?" Jerard looked between me and Shannon.

"Yeah, Persephone told me this morning that you two are together. I had no clue, my bad." I over dramatized it a little, laughing cutely.

"We . . . we're not dating." Jerard pulled his arm away. "Why would you say that?" our group stopped in the hallway, all eyes on Persephone.

"She has a hard time dealing with not getting what she wants." Ryan supplied. "She wanted you, you wanted Claire. She wasn't about to be outdone by the new girl."

"Thanks, Ry." I smirked at him.

"I say it with love." Ryan slipped his arm around my waist again.

"Seph, I thought I explained this to you. You're a great girl but I don't feel that way about you. Let it go." Jerard told her. Persephone stamped her foot and let out a squeal of irritation before taking off in the other direction.

My fifth hour graphic arts class was a whirl wind of safety rules around the machinery and Mr. Dasher's eccentric ramblings. A semester in there was surely going to drive me completely mad, but at least it'd break up the end of the day.

Fifty more minutes and I was free for the day. So far it hadn't been the worst day in the first-day-of-school history. Persephone and Bianca were the only real problems I had. My classes weren't horrible, it was a given that math would always be mind numbing, but I was ready to go home and relax. It could have been a lot worse but it wasn't possible to have anymore drama, or so I thought.

"New girl." I recognized her voice right away. I sighed and turned to face Persephone, she was quickly becoming my biggest pain as well as my arch enemy. I spun angrily.

"What?"

"Just so you know, Jer is *mine*. So you better find someone else to go after." She was taller than me – everyone seemed to be taller than me – but she didn't scare me.

"Last I knew Jerard wasn't a possession. Maybe that's why your striking out with him. Treating him as one." I crossed my arms in front of me. Persephone's eyes narrowed as she took a step closer to me.

"You can twist words all you want, precious, but if I were you, I'd stay away from him."

"You may have everyone else in this school in your purse but you don't scare me." I glared back at her.

"Just stay away from Jer." she reiterated as I glanced over her shoulder.

"Why don't you let Jerard decide that." I nodded at him.

"Let me decide what?" Jerard touched my shoulder. "Are you okay, Claire?"

"Persephone was just telling me to stay clear of you. I told her we should let you decide." I told him, Persephone looked between us horrified to be caught. Jerard's eyes flashed, his bright blue eyes turned dark. Jerard glared at her before ushering me into the classroom. I fell into a seat near he back of the room and laid my head on the desk, I felt Jerard pass me and sit in the seat behind me.

"Only an hour left." Jerard said bracingly.

Our teacher Mrs. Lancaster called our attention to the front of the class. She was younger than most of the teachers and seemed very eager to teach. Which she made very apparent in her first address to us.

"Good afternoon class!" she boomed clasping her hands in front of her, "I'm Mrs. Lancaster and I'll be your history teacher for the year. I'm really excited to get to know you and watch you grow as students this year!" Jerard leaned forward again and whispered in my ear, "Apparently *she* got enough sleep." I stifled a laugh as Mrs. Lancaster went on.

"We're not going to jump into the book right away. With the festival so close I thought we'd start out with a local history project, to ease back into school life. So I want you all to pair up and come see me for a topic." with that she left us to our own devices. I turned and looked at Jerard.

"Hey Claire, hey, wanna be partners? Do ya, do ya, do ya?" Jerard asked me in mock enthusiasm.

"You stay here, I don't want you to break an ankle skipping up to her desk." I laughed at him. I got out of my seat and joined the line at her desk, two people stood in front of me. I waited as Mrs. Lancaster talked to the students in front of me. She seemed to have grown up in the area and was talking to them about their families. I zoned out looking around the room. Posters covered everything from the checks and balances of government to Abraham Lincoln, the one I was currently reading.

"Miss?"

"Sorry," I stepped forward, "I was bonding with Honest Abe."

"Ah, yes, our dear sixteenth president, so much prestige, so much conspiracy." I stared at her, but she didn't elaborate.

"You are?" she asked.

"Claire Weston." I replied, she marked my name off on a list.

"And your partner is?"

"Jerard Lane."

"You look really familiar Claire, do I know you're parents?"

"I don't know, maybe? My mom is – well – was Amelia Kelly." Her eyes lit up inexplicably.

"Oh, well I have the perfect topic for you." she smiled, "Fiona's disappearance. Next."

Confused and thrown off by my abrupt dismissal, I stepped around the girl behind me and made my way back to my desk. I sat, half turned towards Jerard in my seat.

"That's an awfully confused look for having no numbers involved." Jerard mentioned, a half hearted smile playing at his lips. I shook my head trying to get my head back on straight.

"Uh, sorry, she said something about the Fiona Disappearance."

"Oh that's easy." he sat back. "So do we have the hour to just chill out?"

"I guess?" I shrugged, "What's the Fiona Disappearance?"

"This girl back in the fifties disappeared. No one knows what happened to her." Jerard stretched his arms behind him.

"What was her name?"

"Fiona." he stared at me for a moment and then grinned. I rolled my eyes at him.

"Ha ha, her last name funny man."

He chuckled, "Kelly, her name was Fiona Kelly. Everyone knows that story . . . what's wrong, Claire? You look like you've seen a ghost." It was true, my face had fallen and I'd probably dropped a shade or two in tone.

"I . . . Jer will you come over after school? I think you need to see something."

He looked at me strangely for a moment but agreed. We spent the rest of the hour playing Dots, you know that little game where you put dots on the paper and try to make boxes? The one the with the most boxes wins? And talking about 'The Festival' that Mrs. Lancaster had mentioned. Apparently it's actually The Harvest Festival that's held in Old Town every fall. There's food, games, old time photos, live music and dancing. It was this Saturday night, and according to Jerard the whole town turned out for it. He also told me that it was something that Shannon and Ana were probably going to drag me to. The bell was about to ring when he beat me at Dots. I have to admit my heart really wasn't in it. Our topic was bugging me a lot and I tried not to let on, but I failed as we were walking out the door.

"Watch out!" Jerard grabbed my shoulder and held me back as I was narrowly missed by an A/V cart with a blind driver. "You okay?"

Thrown but not shaken, I nodded and headed off to my locker. Jerard cast furtive glances at me as we walked but didn't press anything. The combination was being fickle on my locker, having to spin it several times before the locker gods decided I could get the books I needed for my homework. I sighed, shutting my locker and made to follow Jerard, but he didn't budge. He pressed me against my locker one hand on either side of me. My breath caught in my chest and the after school chatter was reduced to a dull murmur as he stared down at me. He wasn't angry, his icy eyes were full of warmth and concern actually.

"What's wrong?" He whispered, and even though in any other situation I couldn't have heard anything he uttered but his voice rang out as clear as a fire truck siren. My mouth worked, but nothing came out at first.

"It's the project. I have a bad feeling about it is all." I finally managed after a moment. His eyebrows raised curiously, but we were interrupted before he could ask anything.

"Hey you two, these public displays of affection have to stop." The moment was broken, and we looked around to find Shannon beaming with a very stern faced Aiden. Jerard took a step back and glanced at me before turning to Aiden and Shannon.

"I'm going your way, want a ride? Aiden said your car wouldn't start this morning?" he asked them.

"Yeah, stupid car. Thanks, Jer." Shannon replied, "We'll meet you in the lobby, come on Aiden." with that she grabbed his hand and pulled him off. Jerard and I looked at each other, he ran his hand through is hair nervously, and I cleared my throat.

"I-I guess we should get moving."

"Yeah." He retorted, pivoted and I followed silently behind. We were standing at his locker when he spoke again. "Sorry about that. At your locker – I'm usually not that forceful. Shannon usually calls me a teddy bear."

I was leaning against the locker next to his. Surprised at his comment, I tilted my head at him for a moment. I tried to wrap my head around the fact that he thought he'd done something wrong, though it was clear that he had the best of intentions.

"You weren't. I know you meant well." I replied, I added that I didn't mind in and undertone. I saw him glance at me with a smile.

In the lobby Shannon held back to walk with me as Aiden fell into step next to Jerard. There were few words passed between them, but I could tell Aiden was telepathically screaming at him. When we got to the Jeep Jerard helped me into the backseat as Shannon climbed in on the other side. If not for the music the ride would have been silent. The atmosphere in the car was mixed. Jerard and I were trying to be indifferent but beside me Shannon was positively buzzing, and Aiden's jaw was twitching every so often. There was no doubt that he was on the brink of explosion.

Jerard pulled up to the curb, and we all jumped out. Ahead of us on the path to the house, Shannon looped her arm in Aiden's muttering something to him, probably trying to calm him down. Jerard and I fell behind, his hands shoved in his pockets, mine fiddling with the strap on my messenger bag.

"I thought for sure he was going to freak out." Jerard muttered to me.

"Me too."

Inside we found Aiden and Shannon in the kitchen with Mom, Landon and Sam.

"Aww, its so cute you cook together." Shannon smiled sitting at the bar with Aiden. Mom and Landon smiled at her as Jerard and I sat in the other two spots.

"It's not really cooking Shan, its more like cutting and throwing." Aiden actually managed to smile. She rolled her eyes at him.

"How was school?" Mom handed me a chunk of apple. I munched on it as Shannon launched into a long winded play-by-play of *everything* that happened at ASH that day. I caught Jerard's eye and he feigned falling asleep. I put my head down a little to hide my laughter.

"Anyway," I ignored Shannon, turning to Sam. "How was school for you?"

"It was okay." Sam shrugged.

"That doesn't sound good." Jerard chimed in. Apparently the only ones interested in Shannon's account of the day were Aiden, mom and Landon. To be honest, the ones who couldn't get away. Sam shifted uncomfortably.

"Come on." I told Sam, "Let's go in the living room." Jerard and Sam followed me, going unnoticed by anyone else in the room.

"What's up?" Jerard asked as Sam fell onto the couch.

"I hate seventh grade."

"Why?" I asked as Jerard sat next to him, I sat on the coffee table in front of him.

"Stupid people."

" . . . Go on." I tiled my head at him. He looked embarrassed.

"The other guys make fun of me. Especially in gym." Sam revealed finally.

"Why?" Jerard looked like he was trying to hold back a smirk.

"Because I'm smaller than everyone else. You know I'm no good at sports. But do you think any of those guys could . . . could design a casing to drop an egg off the roof and have it not break?"

"A . . . what?" I looked at him in surprise.

"He's talking about the Egg Drop." Jerard told me.

"Yeah, every year we have to design a way to drop and egg off the roof and have it land safely and unbroken." Sam went on.

"Sam's done it successfully three years in a row." Jerard finished.

"Oh."

"So what happened in gym?" Jerard went on.

"We played baseball. My teacher had to put me on a team cause no one wanted me. And then put me at second base. I told them not to even let me play! But a lot of runs happened because of me. And the whole team got mad, because the losers had to run laps at the end of class." Sam looked positively miserable by this point.

"Well." I said bracingly. "Look at it this way Sammy. Those guys are good at sports. If they keep doing well maybe they'll get a scholarship to a college or something that depends on their ability to play."

"Thanks Claire." He glared at me.

"You didn't let me finish. But you'll get an academic scholarship. You'll always be smart, whereas if they get hurt and can't play anymore they'll have nothing to fall back on. So they're better at sports than you are. When they are in danger of getting thrown off the team because they can't keep their grades up. Who do you think they'll be coming to?"

"Me."

"That's right. It sucks that they taunt you the way they do. But remember Sammy, you have something they'll never have. The ability to think logically."

"Thanks, Claire." he said a little more happily this time.

"And you'll probably be taller than them some day. Look how tall Landon and Aiden are. Some guys just grow later on in life." Jerard tacked on. "There's nothing wrong with you."

"Yeah, you're right. Did you know that genetics aren't the only thing that effects height? I mean Dad is tall but Mom wasn't much taller than Claire is. And doctor's can now take a guess at the height of a person between childhood and puberty. But science is ever expanding on the Nature vs. Nurture debate. They're saying that a child who is raised in a loving, bright and airy home is more likely to grow to their full potential. But children raised in dark and dreary atmospheres, I mean literally dark and dreary, it effects not only their mental state of well being but their physical make up too. Besides, there are jobs in the world that are actually size discriminate. Take jockeys for example! Someone Jer's size would be turned away, but guys my size, they're just what people are looking for. Even in more mainstream sports, being smaller is a plus when you want someone who is quick . . ." Sam rambled on as he got up and headed up stairs promising to return with a reference book.

I could tell he was feeling better, even if it meant we'd have to look at whatever book he was bringing back. We were about to go back into the kitchen when we almost ran into Landon in the entryway.

"You guys take the cake." He told us fondly. Jerard and I stared at him.

"You know he wouldn't have taken that as well from Aiden or me." Landon went on.

"Sammy's a good kid." I shrugged. "And I think I just figured out the issues between Sam and Aiden."

"Yeah," Landon nodded thoughtfully, "Aiden's always been a bit intimidated by his younger brother's intelligence. He gets that from this mother. Bright as a penny, Marion was. Completely book smart, though she left a lot to look for in common sense." Landon shook head.

Jerard and I shifted feeling a bit uncomfortable.

"Aiden's a C student, but he did manage to get my common sense." Landon tacked on looking a bit more cheery.

"Come on Claire, girl time!" Shannon appeared in the hallway.

"There's a party in the hallway." Aiden chirped, staring at Jerard. I sighed and followed Shannon up the stairs, leaving Jerard to Aiden. I was sure there were things they were going to have to talk about.

Shannon closed the door behind me and jumped on my bed, looking at me expectantly.

"What?"

"You have got to be kidding me." she drew out each word. "You, Jer, inches apart in the hallway . . . not ringing a bell?" I fell on to the bed next to her.

"Okay, yeah *that* rings a bell." I smiled sheepishly.

"So . . . ?" she nodded slowly.

"Shan, I'm gonna level with you." I told her frankly. "I have no idea what that was about. He was worried about me, but yeah the way he did it, surprised me too."

"But he was *so* close to you!" she hissed.

"Uh, yeah I know! I was there." I reminded her. "He wasn't going to start making out with me right there in the hallway if that's what you're thinking. And if he was, you kinda blew that for me."

"Yeah, didn't think about that." Shannon nodded after a moment.

"Aiden will screw it up for me anyway."

"I'll make sure he doesn't. Jer hasn't dated anyone in a long time." Shannon patted me on the arm. "Speaking of which, I should go and break up that little chat session." without another word she got up and left the room. I was laying on my back staring up at my canopy when Jerard entered the room.

"Aiden's not happy." he fell on to his stomach next to me.

"You think?" I turned my head towards him. "I'm sure somewhere in his brain there's a vein in danger of exploding." Jerard smiled at me.

"What'd he say?" I turned on my side to face him properly.

"That if I valued our friendship I'd stay away from you." he replied, I closed my eyes in exasperation.

"You better clear out then." I said softly, I felt his hand brush some of my hair out of my face and my eyes fluttered open.

"I'll take my chances." he told me, his own hair was falling into his eyes, but there was no doubt of his sincerity. I cleared my throat and nodded, he didn't drop his gaze, and I couldn't find it in me to look away either.

"I feel strangely drawn to you, even if I didn't like who you are, I know I'd still follow you anywhere." Jerard went on. "I can't figure out why." You could hear a pin drop in my room at that moment.

"So what about this project do you have a bad feeling about?" he asked finally. I snapped out the little world I'd gone to and sat up. I didn't reply but got up and rummaged through an old trunk at the end of my bed. It belonged to my Grandfather, and was full of old family stuff. I sifted through the things until I found what I was looking for. A photograph in a silver frame.

"The girl's name was Fiona Kelly?"

"Yeah, why?" Jerard leaned up on his elbows. I bit my lip and moved around the posts to kneel next to him.

"Is this her?" I turned the photo around to show him.

"Hey! That is her, where'd you get that?" Jerard took the photo from me, and my heart and stomach sank. "That'll be great to use in our project."

"Jerard." He looked up at me in question. I closed my eyes again thinking this couldn't be happening.

"My name is Claire Fiona Kelly Weston. Fiona Mary Kelly," I nodded to the photo, "Was my aunt." I saw Jerard look between the photograph and myself and realization seemed to strike in his mind as he started to noticed the family resemblance. "Mom said she died, that she had been really sick, not that she had disappeared."

"Aunt Ona." He nodded. "That's not all that's weird, Claire." He looked closer at the photo.

"What?"

"That's my grandpa, James Davenport." *Oh my god, James! How could I have missed it?!*

Jerard had gone with Aiden and Shannon to a little ice cream shop called Icy Sweets in Old Town. I decided to go for a walk trying to sort out all the things that were bombarding my brain.

School wasn't as bad as it could have been. Persephone is a pain in the ass, Jerard's just as confusing as any boy could be, Mrs. Lancaster is a freaking psycho. I told her mom was a Kelly. Who in their right mind would assign her niece to do a project on her missing aunt – who mom always told me was dead actually. What was with that? Why had Mom and all the others lied to me? Did any of my cousins know that Aunt Fiona could be still living? Had they given up hope after so long? What if she was living in Japan? Okay maybe not Japan but she can't have just disappeared like that. No one can just disappear they have to be somewhere. Where was Aunt Fiona? Was she still here? Dead as everything suspects? Is she in another state? Did she have a family somewhere? Why would she cut ties with us though? And what about James for that matter? If everything I'd seen was true – it looked like they were in love. Though if you ask any adult they'd say there was no way it could have been true love, but what do adults know about teenage emotion? Yeah, yeah they were teenagers once too but times have changed from Aerosmith and . . . and . . . I don't know 21 Jump Street. Did she just leave James and never looked back? What did James do? Did he try to find her? Is he the reason she left? But what if she is dead? What could have happened to her? This is a small town someone had to know something.

"That's a pretty serious look." A voice echoed in my ear. I shook my head clear of thoughts.

"Hey Key. Sorry just thinking." I shrugged.

"Looked important." Key observed.

"Kind of? I don't know." I sighed trying to remember if I actually had a point to begin with.

"What about?"

"Just school is all."

"Ah, how are you liking ASH?" he nodded knowingly.

"Tough to tell right now. Could go either way."

"We've made a great impression on you, haven't we?" He grinned at me.

I laughed, "Just certain aspects. Teachers, students, assignments."

"Let me guess, Mrs. Lancaster and Persephone Adams?"

"How did you know?"

"Persephone made it pretty clear in our last hour English class that she plans to make your life here miserable, she was telling everyone what happened outside of you're history class and she has Mrs. Lancaster wrapped around her finger."

"Great. First day and I've made an enemy."

"I wouldn't worry, Persephone doesn't like anyone." Key grinned at me. "It kind of works both ways."

"I'm not surprised. What are you doing here?" I went on.

"It's a free park." He smiled at me. "Actually, having a sort of family gathering." He motioned off to his left, but I saw no one.

"Are they ghosts?" I raised a brow at him.

"Something like that." He laughed, "Come on." Key shoved his hands in his pockets and led the way across the grass and into a wooded area. The further we went the woods the louder it got. I looked at Key as the voices and distant beats got louder.

"We're a bit noisy, that's why we're all the way out here." Key gave a slightly crooked grin. We came upon the clearing quite suddenly, Key's family, who were also quite blatantly native, were gathered there. There was group of men singing around a drum, women and children listening and doing their own crafts near by.

"Who is this, Kiowa?" a silver haired man asked.

"This is my friend, Claire, Grandfather." Key spoke in such a different tone that I almost didn't recognize him.

"Welcome, Claire." Key's grandfather addressed me.

"Thank you, sir." I nodded politely, he gave off an aura that commanded respect.

"My family and I are having a cultural awakening. We have it once a year to remind us of our ancestors and their trials." His grandfather went on.

"I don't mean to intrude." I took a step back.

"No, my dear girl," His grandfather came to me, "Please, stay and learn. You are welcome among us." Key's grandfather guided me into the clearing and sat me among the women sitting in a circle weaving baskets. Key sat nearby as his aunt and cousin taught me how. I watched another pair of smaller cousins speak to each other in fluent Ojibwe and others dance as the men sang.

It was a culture shock from my very Irish up bringing but interesting none the less. It was nearing dusk when the family started to pack up and go home. Key was about to take me home when his grandfather stopped us.

"Claire, did you enjoy yourself tonight?" he asked.

"Yes, sir. Thank you for letting me stay." I smiled.

"You're welcome to join us anytime." He nodded, "Our culture is nearly forgotten, or made a mockery. The more people who understand us, the better." I nodded and allowed Key to lead me back to the main part of Alden City Park

"Kiowa? Your family is awesome, by the way." I mentioned to him as what was left of the sun fell freely on us again.

"My full name, it means principle people or something. And yeah sometimes they're pretty cool." Key's hands were in his pockets again. "Grandfather takes it a little far, Dad too. Says we're supposed to be proud Anishanabe, but Dad always makes sure that I know the statistics of Native Americans."

"Statistics?"

"Alcoholism, suicide rate, lack of future in general." he shrugged.

"Oh."

Key didn't stay long, something seemed a bit off about him, but he was singing along with the men and even dancing some so I figured he was tired. I wasn't feeling particularly social though, so avoiding Aiden's room all together, where Mom had told me Shannon and Jerard were, I grabbed my math book and headed to the front porch to start on my homework. I *hated* math with a passion, but thankfully our homework was just a few worksheets reviewing pre-algebra.

"What are you doing out here?" Sam came out onto the porch.

"Pre-algebra." I shoved the book aside.

"Oh that's not bad." Sam leaned over looking at the book. "Where have you been? I haven't seen you since the living room."

"I ran into Key at the park. He was having a sort family reunion."

"Did you know that the Ojibwe were incredible warriors? They were one of the most feared tribes in the area. They made treaties with the French and that alone gave them so much power because of the trade. Through the years the tribe has had its ups and downs with the success of their enterprises. The casinos of course, but their Pow Wows are amazingly popular. Though these days the tribe is in debt, a lot of debt but you know they're working to make their nation as proud as it once was."

"How do you remember all this?" I looked up at him.

Sam shrugged and walked back into the house. Reluctantly, I went back to the math.

"So . . . should we ask Mrs. Lancaster to switch the topic?" Jerard asked a few minutes later.

"I'm never going to get this done." I closed the book and tossed it to the other end of the porch. Jerard watched it go, with a sort of amusement playing at the corner of his lips. "I doubt she would let us, she knows who our families are. She must have been pretty set on giving it to us. We just made it easier by pairing up." I looked at him properly for the first time.

"Yeah. Well where do you want to start?" he pushed his bangs out of his face.

"I don't know. I'll think about it tonight. I don't know if I'm even going to tell my mom about this."

"Would she freak out?"

"Probably. Going home? I hope you're mom doesn't get too mad that you've spent the whole day here." I shrugged.

"She won't, she's not there, remember? Her and Dad are on a dig in Egypt."

"Dig?" I got up and followed Jerard to his Liberty.

"They're archeologists."

"You could crash here sometimes?" I suggested, knowing that Landon loved Jerard. He shrugged.

"I'll see you tomorrow, Claire."

I was laying in the hammock on the front porch around two o'clock. After tossing and turning for hours on end, I decided to get up. The end of summer breeze was still warm and it seemed to help me clear my head at least. The crickets were loud. I couldn't believe how loud they were when you stopped to listen. The tranquil and soothing sounds the night were suddenly shattered as I heard a car door slam. My head popped up and I stared into the darkness. I'm kind of weird, I don't fear the dark, it's what I can't see that's in the dark, and right now I couldn't see anything with the porch light on. I heard the footsteps on the pavement and fear started to rise in me. Faceless feet scraped against the pavement. I sat up, poised to make a mad dash for the door, until he stepped into the pale yellow light of the street lamp.

"Jerard?" I started walking towards him. "What are you doing here? You scared the hell out of me."

"Couldn't sleep, so I decided to go for a drive. I ended up here." he shrugged as we met in the middle of the front pathway. "I'd never mean to scare you. Sorry."

"Oh. It's okay." I looked right into his chest, straying as quick as possible from his eyes.

"Wanna come for a ride with me?" he lifted my chin with his index finger. I stood frozen for a moment, all the confusion and drama from the last day seemed to have melted away.

"No way, its two in the morning. What if mom and Landon wake up? I'll be toast." I shook my head.

"They'll never know. Come on." Jerard took my hand and turned his body towards the street but didn't take a step. He gave me a buoyant grin and I sighed giving in. I had a feeling I'd have a hard time saying no to Jerard in the future.

The streets of Alden's Hollow were empty, the old fashioned street lamps giving off an almost ghostly glow. It was so peaceful that I couldn't imagine anything bad ever happening to anyone. Yet something *had* happened to Aunt Ona.

I wasn't surprised when we ended up at the park, it was one of the few places we could roam freely with out people wondering why two teenagers were out at 2:30 in the morning. Our conversation was easy, but meaningless. About school and pets, friends and hobbies.

"Have you been to the cliffs yet?" Jerard asked as we pulled into the park.

"The cliffs?"

"They're on the edge of the lake."

"Oh, no I haven't been to the lake yet." I shook my head, Jerard smiled and took another road within the park.

I was surprised to find that the park was much more than just the well manicured lawns with play grounds and barbeque pits. There was a whole other world of overgrown foliage that I hadn't seen yet, with a small one-way road winding through it. I had to admit it was a little creepy out here at night. Like something out of one of those horrible slasher films that Aiden was so fond of, but beautiful and peaceful in its own right.

If I'd been driving, I would have missed the driveway all together. It was kind of hidden within the bushes on either side, but Jerard hit it expertly, we followed it down a little bit and parked in a surprisingly big parking area. There were no other cars, but the second I stepped out I could hear the water. I waited for Jerard to lead the way and soon I found myself picking my way over large boulders and other sharper rocks. I was usually cautious about touching Jerard after our last few encounters but I didn't hesitate to reach out for him whenever I felt like I was going to fall. If it weren't for the moonlight I would have been completely blind but I could still hear Jerard chuckle a little each time.

"Shut up, Jerard." I laughed, "Rocks and accident prone people don't mix."

"Okay, okay. I'll be good." I stopped suddenly.

"What is it?"

"She was here." I gulped, I couldn't explain it, but I felt my Aunt here.

"Here? At the cliffs?" I nodded, reaching out for him.

The sky was gray and it was misting but Fiona was reasonably dry hugging a coat to her. She looked out over the lake, a sadness tugging at her eyes that clearly ended deep within her heart. James was nowhere in sight, and I knew instantly the source of the sadness. She didn't care that she was beginning to look like a drown rat rather than the beautiful young girl I knew her to be, I could tell all she worried about was James. What he was doing, and if he was safe. With one last look to the horizon Fiona started slowly back across the slippery rocks, but instead of taking the trail to the parking lot, she took another into the woods. The mist didn't fall here, too many trees crowded together for that, but it was just as dark and dreary. Or maybe it was just her mood reflecting on everything around her. The last glimpse of Fiona was her slipping into the black arch in a large rock face.

"Damn it." Jerard's voice broke in my ear. "I hate it when that happens."

"It throws me for a loop too." I admitted touching my head feeling that all too familiar dizziness.

"What is the deal with that? Why does this happen to us?" He demanded, but softened his tone when he saw my own helpless look.

"I don't know." I shrugged sitting on the closest boulder. "Maybe because we're relatives? Maybe Aunt Fiona and your grandpa are trying to help us find her . . . as far fetched as that sounds."

"I-well – I guess that could be happening, I guess." he said skeptically.

"And maybe the reason we see them the way we do is cause we're blood. Maybe its some weird twist of fate, but either way, I think my Aunt's been waiting a long time to be found and I'm taking every advantage I can to find her." Jerard still looked skeptical but nodded. "I'll do every thing I can to help you."

TUESDAY

THE ALARM FOR six thirty came all too quickly and I had a rough time getting up and going. Instead of searching my closet for a cute outfit I opted for jeans and a hoodie that showed my support for my favorite major league soccer team, the New England Revolution.

"Jer's here." Sam said from the doorway.

"I'll be down in a few." I yawned stuffing my math book back in my messenger bag. Jerard looked worse than I did with dark circles under his eyes and even his bright blue eyes seemed duller.

"You two look horrible." Aiden commented upon my arrival.

"You really know how to charm a girl, Aiden."

"Ask Shannon, she'll tell you that I'm really good at compliments." Aiden returned.

"We're going now mom." Jerard and I forced a laugh before leaving the house.

"Are you okay to drive?" I looked at him as he held the door of the Liberty open for me.

"I'm okay." He nodded half heartedly.

Alden Senior High was less intimidating today. Jerard parked in the student lot and led the way into the school trying to stay awake by talking about something his parents had found on their dig. I didn't have the heart to tell him that I was only catching every third word or so. We wandered until we found Ryan and Key near Key's locker sitting in those foldable camp chairs.

"Very nice guys." I nodded approvingly, sitting with my back against the wall across from them. Ryan and Key grinned back at me.

"Did either of you sleep last night?" Key's hair was pulled back in a half ponytail today. "You both look like you haven't slept in days."

"Not really." Jerard sat next to me.

"No more caffeine for you after eight pm." Ryan instructed.

"Thank you, Dr. Winters." I mumbled leaning my head on Jerard's shoulder, assuming that if we were being taken hostage by our deceased relatives that we'd be too tired to be thrown off by it.

"The bill's in the mail." Ryan retorted playfully. "But, I'd be more than willing to make a house call for you . . ." I hid my eyes into Jerard's shoulder thinking how horrible our jokes were this early in the morning. Jerard slid an arm around my back allowing me to move into a more comfortable position. The next thing I knew the bell was ringing and Jerard was gently shaking me awake.

"Time for class." he muttered to me.

"No." I returned. "Sleep." He laughed helping me up.

Jerard's head was on his desk when I walked into math. I knelt down next to his desk and leaned mine on it too.

"Hey, sleeping beauty." I said softly. Jerard's head popped up, and he ran a hand through his hair to get it out of his face.

"Hey," he said sleepily.

"You didn't sleep at all last night, did you?" I slipped into the seat behind him and pulling out last night's homework.

"Uh, no, not really." He slowly turned to face me.

"Why not? I passed out the second I hit the pillow" Jerard furrowed his brow for a moment and looked around as if he didn't want to heard. I looked around with him and leaned towards him.

"I kept having nightmares." he muttered staring me straight in the eye, as if daring me to laugh.

"What about?" I asked composedly.

Mr. Goetz cleared his throat and we all fell silent. I didn't even bother paying attention today. I knew Jerard would be better at explaining it than Goetz would be anyway. So I sat and wrote a mini biography on myself for my English class. Fifteen minutes before the bell I slipped my biography away as Mr. Goetz was coming around with today's worksheet.

"So tell me about these . . . dreams." I leaned forward, knowing that he wouldn't want to talk about it at lunch. Jerard's eyes narrowed at those around us for a minute, but I guess he was satisfied that we weren't worth listening to and leaned closer to me as well.

"I was at war." He replied softly, "The first one, I was getting off the plane and I was led to this place where they gave us our gear, you know, guns, duffle bags? That stuff. Anyway we went through this place and there was a sign over the entry way. It said 'The best damn soldiers in the world come through this door.' Just after we walked through the door I was in a jeep with two other guys and we were under fire. When we got out of danger I noticed a bullet hole in the seat barely an inch from my ribs. That was the first time I woke up." I nodded him on, he cast another furtive glance around be started again.

"The second one, I was sitting in a hole with four other guys playing cards and I guess I got out to go to the bathroom. When I jumped back down into the hole I found three of them with surprised looks on their faces, the last guy didn't even have the chance to look up. Claire, they were dead, all of them." I bit my lip, that was kinda bad.

"And the last." he shuddered a little, "The last one, it was winter, our squad was making its way though a field. The guy in front of me was a ways ahead of the rest of us. I was goofing off with the guy next to me, and we were catching up with him. Then it all happened so fast. There was an explosion, and the next thing I know, I'm picking pieces of flesh and bone off of me." I cringed at that thought and understood his lack of sleep completely.

"Yeah, that's what I did too." Jerard noticed my reaction. We both jumped violently as the bell sounded forgetting for a moment where we were. Jerard sighed, pushed his hair back and stood up. I looked up at him helplessly. He was always carelessly handsome but today Jerard just looked . . . depressed.

"Two more hours." he extended a hand to me. I took it and he helped me out of his seat.

"Two more hours." I nodded.

Shannon and Ana were nearly bursting when Jerard and I ran into them in the commons few minutes later.

"Can we steal her?" Ana grabbed my arm.

"Go ahead." He shrugged, and headed into the lunchroom alone. I followed Shannon and Ana into a less populated area of the commons and they turned to me.

"Is he okay?" Shannon asked as I crossed my arms in front of me almost physically chilled by his nightmares.

"Yeah, he's not been sleeping well is all." I replied, "What's going on?"

"Declan Sullivan just asked me to the Festival!" Ana said excitedly. I stared between the two confused.

"Declan is this guy she's had a crush on since like eighth grade. The guy she was telling you about at my house?" Shannon explained.

"Oh!" realization hit, "Well done, Ana."

"Thanks! I'm so excited!"

"There's our lovely ladies." Key greeted us as we wandered into the cafeteria finally, "Ryan thought you'd all gotten better offers."

"Hey Key," I sat between him and Jerard. "Ana did, but you're still stuck with Shan and I."

"What?" All the boys looked up at Ana in particular.

"Claire!" she looked embarrassed.

"A boy, who shall remain nameless to protect Ana from being ridiculed, asked her to the festival. End of story, leave her alone about it." I told them all as Shannon and Ana left to get food.

"Who is it?" Ryan leaned in.

"It's Ana's secret, ask her." I shrugged.

"Aww," Ryan leaned back disappointed. "You're supposed to be our eyes and ears into the other side, Claire."

"So am I your man behind enemy lines?" I raised a brow at them. Ryan, Key and Jerard looked at each other.

"I think we would all agree that you're not a man." Ryan nodded thoughtfully. "Guys?"

"I agree completely." Key nodded.

"Yeah, I would say she's too soft and bumpy, Jer?" Ryan went on, Jerard just grinned at me choosing not to get involved.

"Soft and bumpy?" I was slightly amused. "Wow Ry, you really know how to make a girl feel special."

"Its a gift he has." Jerard took a drink of his chocolate milk.

"Hey come on." Aiden seemed grossed out by the conversation.

"The conspicuous absence of a girlfriend is now understood." I winked at Jerard, completely ignoring my stepbrother.

"Hey." Ryan chimed, "Too many girls to choose just one."

"You'd have to find one who could stand you first, man." Key mentioned.

"Come on, what girl wouldn't want some of this?" Ryan flexed for us. "Claire?"

"You wouldn't like my answer." I laughed.

To my surprise, neither Key or Ryan bugged Ana about her mystery date. I was willing to bet that they were waiting for me to tell Jerard and get it out of him. Key and Ryan continued their playful banter as Jerard and I tore into our own sack lunches.

"You better watch your back Claire." Aiden told me through a mouthful of pizza.

"Why?"

"Persephone's on the warpath and it leads straight to you." Aiden replied.

"Yeah. She's going pretty crazy about you and Jer." Ryan went on. "I'm sure you had a Persephone in Oakdale."

"Oh, yeah every school has one. But she wasn't going after me." I shrugged trying not to look too bothered by it. Truth be told I could care less about Persephone, but the stigma from it all was sure to have repercussions that weren't needed.

"So, Ana found a really great DJ for the party!" Shannon returned sitting next to Ryan, "And Mom's got a food list made up. Everything's coming together awesomely. Now girls," Shannon went on exiling the boys for a moment, "We need to go shopping for outfits!"

"We do?" I looked up at her, "Didn't we just do school shopping? And isn't it a pool party?"

"No one actually swims at a pool party." Shannon told me plainly. "Are you really passing on a trip to go shopping?"

"No one swims at a pool party? Doesn't that kind of defeat the purpose?" I stared around at Key, Ryan, Aiden and Jerard.

"We're not in it." Ryan backed away.

"Chickens." I grinned at them, "Shan, I still have clothes I haven't worn from school shopping yet. I do not need to go shopping."

"But, we have to accessorize." Shannon told me as if I should have known this all along.

"I don't wear accessories, I wear my Claddagh, that's it. Count me out." I shook my head.

"You're not fun, Claire." Shannon sighed taking a bite of her pizza.

"I know, I know." I grinned at Jerard.

The girls fell into an easy conversation about their shopping trip they planned to take, and let me know quickly that they intended to drag me along. Meanwhile the boys talked over the chances ASH had at winning the first football game of the season against Livingston on Friday night.

"Will you come over after school again?" I asked Jerard as we got rid of our trays.

"Sure, why?"

"I found some newspaper clippings and photos in that trunk last night about Aunt Fiona's disappearance. We should probably get to work on this project."

"Are you going to be okay with this?" Jerard looked grave. "We can try to get it switched, if you want."

I shook my head, "No, I have to try to figure out what happened to her."

"What are you two muttering about?" Ryan dumped his tray as well.

"That whole Fiona Kelly thing." Jerard explained. "We have to do a project on it."

"Oh, cool." Ryan nodded, "Did you guys get to Richard Taylor yet?"

"Who?" we chorused.

"That's the guy they pinned it on. He went to prison for it." Ryan asked. "You didn't come across him yet?"

"No . . ."

"Yeah, something about a conspiracy? I don't know, he was a little off his nut. Mrs. Lancaster never really got over it, or so I've heard." Ryan shrugged casually.

"Wait, what does Mrs. Lancaster have to do with it?" Jerard quizzed.

"Richard Taylor was Mrs. Lancaster's dad." Ryan could have hit me with a brick and I wouldn't have been as surprised.

"What?" Ryan looked at me.

Jerard and I made our way to History that day, unsure of what to expect from Mrs. Lancaster. She stood outside her doorway watching our classmates like a hawk eyeing its prey.

"She's going to tear into us." I mentioned to Jerard as we drew closer to her.

"No she's not." Jerard took my hand. "I bet she won't even say anything."

"Mr. Lane, Miss. Weston." She folded her arms.

"Mrs. Lancaster." We chimed attempting to go into the classroom, but she stood in the doorway.

"I trust your project is coming along nicely?" she raised a brow. "Finding interesting things?"

"Very well." I nodded, "We're dedicating a whole section to Richard Taylor. A bit of a nut wasn't he? I feel sorry for that man's family. To know they were living with a murderer." I shook my head laying it on thicker than peanut butter. Mrs. Lancaster looked abashed, and if the bell hadn't rang I was sure she would have replied.

"Take your seats." she said tight lipped. She shuffled papers furiously at her desk for a few moments, apparently trying to collect herself.

"You walk on fire, Claire." Jerard muttered to me.

"What's she going to do? Put me in detention for expressing an opinion?" I shrugged.

We spent the first part of class talking about the Civil War, the second half we went to the library to work on our projects. We spread out over the second floor of the library where the books on local stuff were. Mrs. Mackenzie, the librarian milled about helping students where she could. Pointing us in the direction of a rather funny looking machine that apparently held electronic copies of all the old newspapers.

As we browsed through the articles we made notes on a lot of things. For instance that Jerard's grandfather had been the original suspect in her disappearance, that Richard Taylor had been arrested on and anonymous tip to the police from a "very reliable" source, and that he had died in prison in 1978. Among the articles were the obituaries of Richard Taylor, James Davenport, and Henry, Elizabeth and Fiona Kelly. I felt my heart sink the moment I read my mom's name listed under the "Survived by" section. I hadn't really thought about it, but it must have been horrible for mom to lose her sister at such a young age, well to know death at such a young age. If I did the math right, which I probably didn't even my adding and subtracting sucked, Mom only would have been around six.

The bell rang before we knew it, and we were the last to leave as Mrs. Mackenzie was helping us print off a bunch of the articles to work from.

"Funny you should get this assignment, Jerard. Seeing the family connection and all." Mrs. Mackenzie mentioned as I tucked the articles into my notebook.

"More than you know." Jerard nodded, Mrs. Mackenzie looked confused, but didn't press the subject. "Thanks for your help." With that Jerard led the way down the stairs and into the main buildings.

"So lets see if I got this straight." I sighed as we weaved through our classmates. "Your grandpa comes home a hero, purple heart and all. Not long after Aunt Fiona goes missing, they try to blame him, but get info on Taylor and let him go. Claiming they'd never thought it was him to begin with, they never found a body or anything but Taylor gets sent to the big house and dies there. Case closed?"

"Does sound a bit shady, doesn't it?" Jerard nodded as we stopped at his locker.

"A bit." I agreed. "So what's the plan now?"

"No clue. Start writing it?" Jerard shrugged, "I don't think we're going to find her Claire."

"You're giving up easily." I raised a brow.

"Don't look at me like that, I'm not giving up. Just being realistic, you read the articles. They had everyone in the state looking for her. What makes you think we're going to find her?" he chose his words carefully.

"She wants me to find her." I said perhaps a little more defensively than needed, "I can feel it. And you're grandfather's trying to help too. Or else – " I caught myself and lowered my voice. "Or else you wouldn't be having these nightmares."

"I don't know what to think." Jerard replied after a moment. "Its weird that I'm having them, but come on Claire. Trying to talk to us from the grave? That's a bit far fetched."

"Far fetched, but not impossible. I'll do it on my own though. Or I bet Sam would help. He's good at research." I started to walk away.

"Claire, wait." Jerard took a few steps forward and caught my arm. "I didn't say I wouldn't help."

"Let go of me, Jerard." I glared at him, "I'm not going to give up. You can do whatever you want, but there's a reason why when we touch sometimes we see them. There's a reason you're having these dreams and there's a reason it's happening to us. If you're going to be negative about it all then shove off, because I know that the negativity will weaken whatever connection, I or you or we have to the other side."

"Having a lovers quarrel already?" Key appeared next to us.

"Something like that." I jerked my arm out Jerard's hand.

"Oh." Key caught my hostility. "I – um – have to get to – uh. The bus. Yeah the bus, I'll see you guys tomorrow."

I was too irritated with Jerard to really take notice.

"We need Charlie."

"What?" I snapped.

"Charlie Fiske, he was an old army buddy of my Grandpa's, he moved to Alden's Hollow when he got shipped stateside." Jerard looked at his watch. "Wanna go see if he's at the Barrel?"

"What's the Barrel?" I tilted my head at him. "And I thought you didn't believe in all this."

"Never mind you're coming." He shook his head leading the way. "You don't even know what The Barrel is."

Jerard led the way to my locker and I collected my books, before taking my hand and maneuvering through the crowded halls towards the parking lot. Ignoring my last question all together.

Across the aisle Aiden stood at Shannon's car, Shannon chattering away about something, didn't notice the death glare he was using to follow us with. After we dealt with the usual end of the day traffic jam, we found ourselves making our way through Old Town.

"Just wait 'til Christmas." Jerard mentioned I stared out the window, still amazed at how beautiful Old Town was. "Its like something out of a Christmas card." I smiled, "Sounds idyllic."

A few minutes later, we pulled into the parking lot of a very large and old building. It had a hanging sign over the door that showed a maid with a stick stirring what I assumed would be laundry in a barrel. Inside there was a long bar and several old wooden tables with long benches along them. People were drinking from pewter mugs and eating off of glass plates.

"This is great!" I tried to take in my surroundings revolving on the spot. Jerard looked at me with a smile on his face. Probably happy I wasn't angry anymore.

"I didn't think that you'd like it that much." he mentioned surveying the bar. "Come on." he grabbed my hand and pulled me through the crowd of people heading towards the long Oak bar.

"Lane." an ancient looking bartender growled.

"Hey, Pete," Jerard greeted laying a hand on the bar. "We're looking for Charlie, have you seen him?"

"He's over there." Pete the bartender pointed a gnarled finger towards a small seating area near a fireplace.

"Thanks, Pete, come on Claire." he led the way again through the crowd of people towards the fireplace.

"Jerard, m'boy!" a sturdy older man stood to shake hands with him.

"Hi Charlie," Jerard smiled, "Charlie, this is Claire Weston."

"You sure know how to pick 'em, Jerard." he clapped Jerard on the shoulder, "Nice to meet you little lady, say you look really familiar, do I know you're parents?" I could feel myself go red, "Um, maybe. I belong to the Kelly clan, my mom's Amelia." Charlie's buoyant grin faltered a little as his pale brown eyes looked between Jerard and I.

"Oh, yes, I remember Amelia. She was such a happy child. We were sure that she was an alien." Charlie recovered after a moment.

"I often have that same feeling." I smiled at him.

"Sit down, sit down," Charlie motioned to a couch opposite of his cushy armchair. "To what do I owe the pleasure?"

"I came to talk to you about Grandpa." Jerard and I took a seat.

"What about him?"

"We have to do a local history project, our teacher assigned us the Kelly disappearance." Jerard told him.

"What a coincidence." Charlie nodded in my direction.

"Yeah, imagine my surprise to find out that my Aunt is a hometown celebrity." I crossed my arms, "To bad it's because they never found her." Charlie and Jerard looked at me with a sort of pity that made me kind of angry.

"Anyway," I went on, "Jerard found his Grandpa linked to her disappearance, we were wondering what you could tell us."

"Oh Jerard, really . . ." Charlie turned on Jerard.

"Come on, Charlie, you knew him better than anyone, you guys were in the trenches together. He would've died in Korea if not for you. He told us you were the one who carried him to the aid station." Looking slightly mollified, Charlie took a deep breath.

"Your Grandpa loved Fiona, he proposed to her in Korea, and sent her a diamond ring he picked up in Tokyo on leave one time. Fiona said yes, and they planned their wedding for the summer after he got home from Korea. But Fiona was in High school still, so they kept their engagement under wraps until he got home. Their parents knew of course, but Fiona only wore the ring when she was in the house." Jerard and I looked at each other in surprise, we were almost cousins.

"James wrote home from a MASH telling her that he had been wounded, and was coming home very soon. She started making the arrangements for the wedding. Only close friends and family were to be invited. But see, Korea had changed him. He told me that even at Walter Reed he woke up during the night feeling like he was surrounded by the enemy. He didn't sleep well after that." I nudged Jerard, giving him a significant look.

"The thing you have to understand about war is that it's never as great as they say it is in the movies. They capture the action, but never really the heart of it. Imagine, if you will, lying in a fox hole with three of your buddies playing cards, you get up to use the latrine and when you come back all three of your buddies are dead. One of them wearing a surprised look on their face, the other two looking as if the game had never stopped. You're Grandpa went through that, Jerard." Charlie went on as if stopping wasn't an option. I stared at Jerard who shifted uncomfortably.

"The simplest things can trigger a memory or a reaction. In the military you are taught to react first. If you spend too much time thinking, you're going to die, and so is half of your platoon. James came home a changed man, the one constant thing in his life, you're aunt," He nodded to me, "Helped him through it. She comforted him in a way that no one else could. He felt he was responsible for her, his sense of duty and honor was for her. Your Grandpa was at the park with her that night, but he doesn't remember anything that happened after they got to The Cliffs, that's where they think she disappeared." Jerard and I had been listening to intently I hadn't realized that we were both leaning forward hanging on his every word. Jerard let out a low whistle and leaned back against the couch, I rested my head in my hands.

"What happened when they couldn't find Aunt Fiona?"

"James was crushed. No one ever spoke about the wedding again. He waited for her for years, he wanted her to be there, like she always had been. But then you're Grandma came along. Still he always hoped Fiona would come home." Charlie looked really heavy hearted, I could understand why, Jerard's Grandpa had been a good friend. It had to hurt to talk about it, even after all this time. I sat back to think about what I'd heard while Jerard and Charlie turned the conversation to school and family.

"Claire, Claire? Are you ready?" I suddenly realized that Jerard was waving a hand in front of my eyes trying to get my attention.

"What? Oh, yeah, sorry." I apologized getting up.

"It was good to meet you, Claire." Charlie extended a hand to me.

"You too, sir," I shook his hand, "thanks for helping us."

"No problem at all my dear," He waved a hand at me. "Come see us again, and don't you let her get away." he added to Jerard. It was his turn to be embarrassed.

"Bye, Charlie."

We were laughing as we walked up the steps to the house. Despite the fact that some screwed up stuff was going on, Jerard still had a really good sense of humor. We stopped just outside the door and I leaned against the door frame.

"I should probably get home. I start spending too much time over here, Landon might start playing the dad role." Jerard mentioned.

"Sure, leave me alone with Aiden." I smiled at him letting my hair fall into my face. "I'll look through that stuff tonight and bring in anything that looks promising."

"You'll get over it." He reached forward and tucked my hair behind my ear. He lingered on my the ends as the door opened. Surprised Jerard and I looked at the person standing in the doorway, taking a step back. At first Aiden looked as surprised as us, but then his face contorted with anger. He started yelling at Jerard though I couldn't understand what he was saying. I stood rooted on the spot as Aiden started advancing on Jerard who was backing away. It was almost surreal to see six foot tall Jerard backing away from five-foot nine Aiden. On the level, Jerard was lean and Aiden was stocky but still. It was hard to believe he'd shrink away from anyone being as tough as he had to be. I was caught off guard by the whole situation and I couldn't tell you how many blows Aiden got in before I unfroze myself.

"Aiden stop." I pulled at his arm. "What is your problem?" Aiden shoved me away and I hit the side of the house before running inside to find Landon. Who, it seemed like in a matter of seconds, was tearing Aiden away from Jerard. Aiden was heavier than Landon, but not stronger. Landon was barking at Aiden and shoving him into the house. All I managed to catch was

" . . . Your best friend . . . !"

"What the hell was that about?" Jerard was bent over confused. "Did you understand a word he said?" I shook my head at him, I felt stupid when I realized he couldn't see me.

"No." I shook my head as Jerard sat shakily on railing of the porch. His hands were covering his face so anything he said, and he said a lot, came out mumbled.

"Jerard, here," I gently took his wrists in my hands. "Let me look. I can't understand anything you're saying." Jerard allowed me take his hands away and he looked up at me. Aiden had done himself proud. His left eye was starting to swell and there was a small but aggressive cut on his cheek bone.

"That bad?" he gave a lopsided smile. I rearranged my face.

"I'm sorry. I-I, come inside. You're bleeding." I led him into the house, an amused look on whatever parts of his face it didn't hurt to move, and we could hear Landon going through the roof at Aiden in the living room. Mom was standing in the entry way in case Landon needed back up, while Sam sat at the top of the stairs listening carefully with his chin on his knees.

"Sam." Jerard muttered to him, Sam looked up at Jerard and me, "You don't want to be here right now."

Sam nodded and headed back up to his room. We sneaked past Mom into the kitchen and tried to ignore Aiden and Landon fighting in the next room as I got out the first aid kit Mom kept in the kitchen and tended to Jerard's cut. The fight ended in Aiden slamming the door to his room and Landon threatening to take it off the hinges.

"Jerard, honey, are you okay?" Mom crossed her arms in front of her clearly feeling awkward.

"I'm okay, Mrs. Hart." Jerard looked up at her, an ice pack against his eye.

"I don't think Aiden meant what he said." Mom went on.

"Do you know what he said?" we both looked at her curiously.

"We don't speak gibberish." I went on.

"He was jealous." Mom replied, "He thought you were taking Jerard away from him. Aiden asked Jerard to leave you alone but apparently he thought you two were getting too close."

"So he hits him?"

Mom shrugged. "Teenage boys will do weird things."

"My eye feels better." Jerard stood up abruptly, "I think I'll go home."

"Okay." I stood too. He handed me the ice pack which I handed to Mom. I stared at Mom praying she'd get the silent hint I was giving her to leave.

"Oh!" she caught on, "I-umm – better go get dinner started. Call us if you need anything Jerard."

"Thanks, Mrs. Hart." he nodded as she moved over to the refrigerator and we left the house.

"When are your parents coming back?" I bit my lip.

"I don't know." he muttered, "I never know, they just kind of show up once in a while." I looked up at him, his shorter layers falling from behind his ears as he looked back down at me. I always sucked at consoling people. I looked away, angry with myself.

"You have that look again." he whispered placing his hands on my sides and drawing me closer.

"I feel like I'm supposed to say something comforting – but I got nothing." I admitted sheepishly.

"I'm tough." He assured, "My parents haven't been in the picture for a while."

"No one should have to be alone."

"I'm not alone anymore. I'll see you in the morning Claire." Jerard hugged me to him briefly and took off in his jeep.

WEDNESDAY

AIDEN WASN'T TALKING to anyone the next morning, but his anger had several other outlets. I was almost finished getting ready when I heard something fall down the stairs. When I came into the hallway I found it was someone rather than something. Sam was laying at the bottom on the short staircase. Aiden was walking into the kitchen. I took the stairs two at a time until I reached Sam.

"You okay, Sammy?" I leaned down. He looked like he really wanted to cry, but he held back.

"I'm fine." He said gruffly as he allowed me to help him up. In the kitchen Sam was content to let things lie but I was getting too irritated.

"You're such a jerk!" I slapped him across the face.

"Claire!" Mom gasped.

"First Jerard, now your own brother." I ignored Mom. "You need to grow up Aiden. You're pushing everyone close to you away because you can't man up to the fact we're not going anywhere. Do you honestly think Key, Ryan and Ana are going to want to deal with you today once they've seen what you did to Jerard?"

I was prepared for Aiden to take a swing at me, but he didn't. Instead he slouched back in his chair looking sorrowful.

"Can I stay home?" Aiden looked at Landon, who was completely shocked at the scene in his kitchen.

"You most certainly can not." Landon shook his head finding his voice again. Aiden pushed his bowl of cereal away and returned to him room. Mom and Landon stared at me. I didn't know what to do either, so I went back to my room and finished getting ready. Jerard wasn't picking me up that day. He'd texted me last night and told me that he should stay away this morning but he'd see me at school. Sam and I hopped into Mom's car a little while later and headed into town.

"You shouldn't have hit Aiden, Claire." Mom told me as she made her way through the streets.

"Are you kidding? It was amazing!" Sam piped up from the back seat. I saw Mom's mouth twitch, I was sure she was going to smile but she didn't.

"All the same, don't hit your brother." Mom cleared her throat.

"Just push them down the stairs?" I countered.

"That's so much better!" Sam agreed jovially.

"No! Do not push each other down the stairs." Mom replied wearily. Sam and I grinned at each other.

I found Jerard sitting on the stairs outside the side doors when Mom dropped me off. His hair pulled back again in a ponytail, his blue and gray Jansport bag at his feet and those gorgeous eyes covered by large aviator sunglasses. I said goodbye to Mom and made my way towards him.

"So, the sun too bright? Or does your eye look that bad?" I sat beside him.

"A little bit of both I guess." Jerard shrugged.

"Let's see." I requested, his eyes were shaded obviously, but I saw his brow arch a little before pulling off his glasses. His cut looked angry, but healing. His eye however, I was sure would be navy blue with bruise, was only a slate gray. "Oh. I was expecting a lot worse."

"Aiden isn't as tough as he wants everyone to think." Jerard stood and offered me his hand. I smirked taking it as he helped me up.

James stood near a burning barrel warming his hands in the winter chill. His eye swollen shut and purple.

"What happened to you Davenport?" a man who was clearly his superior asked. James stiffened and saluted.

"Nothing sir, just a friendly fight gone awry."

"At ease." the man said. "Another quarrel with Fiske?"

"Sir?"

"It seems that you two have been scuffling quite a bit lately." the man eyed him closely.

"It's a personal matter sir. Nothing to be worried about. I'm sure it will resolve itself." James waived it off.

"Make sure it's soon." the man said menacingly.

"Yes, sir."

"You're never going to want to touch my hands again are you?" I asked him feeling myself released.

"It does seem to happen more that way, doesn't it?" Jerard slid his sunglasses back on. "I'll take my chances though. I like your hands, they're soft."

Turning red I slid on my own off brand sunglasses and followed him into the building. We made our way through the lobby avoiding the large clusters of people and to his locker.

"Key says Mrs. Lancaster is on the warpath." he mentioned spinning the dial.

"That woman is never happy, I'm not worried." I shrugged.

"Secret Agent man, secret agent man, they've given you a number and taken away your name." Ryan sang dramatically coming towards us. I laughed until he grabbed me, and dipped me while he continued to sing. "Beware the pretty faces that you find, a pretty face can hide an evil mind . . ."

"How do you even know the words to that song?" I loosened myself from his clutches.

"My dad is a big fan of stuff like that." Ryan shrugged. "So seriously, what's with the 007 look?"

I glanced at Jerard, who sighed and removed the glasses.

"What the hell happened to you?" Ryan demanded in surprise.

"What was that Mr. Winters?" Mr. Bishop, the principal happened to be walking by.

"Heck, sir, I meant heck." Ryan turned slowly, "But the surprise of the deformity on my friends face shot my normally wholesome speech into something a little more harsh."

Mr. Bishop lingered for a few moments, most likely trying to decide of he was being made fun of, before moving off down the hall. We weren't even sure he was out of ear shot when we all started laughing.

"And you say I walk on fire?" I turned to Jerard. He shrugged, smiling.

"So what happened? Did you beat him up Claire?" Key nudged me playfully.

"*I* didn't beat him up." I watched Jerard shut his locker as we moved along to go to mine.

"Step on a rake?" Ryan supplied falling into step next to him.

"It was Aiden." I said before Jerard to make up an excuse.

"Wait, Aiden hit you? He's your best friend . . . I thought?" Ryan looked between Key and Jerard. They both shrugged.

I'd been pretty lucky to escape Persephone's wrath the day before, but she was more than willing to make up for lost time. Jerard, Key and I were walking into the lunch room when the drama started. Persephone and two of her flying monkeys blocked our path as we made our way to our usual table.

"Oops." was the ominous warning she gave me before proceeding to shove her lunch tray across my chest.

"What the hell, Persephone?!" Jerard roared as I let the tray hit the floor with a surprisingly loud clang, my brilliantly white shirt was now covered in spaghetti.

"Only when you're wearing white." I looked at one of the girls that stood behind Persephone. She looked at me like I was crazy for even looking at her let alone speaking to her directly. It hadn't really hit me until that point that more than half the cafeteria was starting at me. The pure frustration with Persephone sent me over the edge and I felt hot tears start to roll down my cheeks before escaping to the bathroom.

"Claire? Are you in here?" Ana's voice echoed in the empty bathroom.

"Yeah." I sniffed from the opposite end of the room. "I usually don't cry in public. I'm just tired."

"And a mess." Shannon motioned to my shirt.

"Tactful, Shan." Ana glared at her.

"Well it is. That spaghetti sauce will never come out." Shannon stated wide eyed.

"Oh well. I can always get a new shirt." I wiped away the last tear I told myself I would spend on Persephone.

"Jerard's so mad, I've never seen him like this." Ana went on. "Mrs. Harper gave Persephone detention. I guess she thought Mrs. Lancaster was supposed to be monitoring lunch today."

"Good." I felt a bit better knowing that Persephone would be rotting in detention for a while.

"Ana? Shannon? Is she in there?" Jerard's voice came through the doorway. I saw his reflection in the long mirror that faced the door-less entry way.

"Yeah! You can come in Jer, it's just us in here." Shannon replied. I wish I could have seen the internal battle Jerard must have been going through as he hesitated hovering just outside the door.

"I'll wait out here." he said finally.

"Come on, Claire. We'll go to the school store and get you a hoodie." Shannon said bracingly. I nodded and followed her out into the hallway again.

"Have you had enough of today?" Jerard asked me abruptly.

"Yes."

"Lets go then." Jerard motioned to the side door we always came in. I stared between the three of them.

"We can't skip, it's the third day!" I told him.

"You need to learn to live dangerously, Claire. Shan and Ana will cover for us won't you?" Jerard looked at him.

"Yeah, what's your locker combination? We'll get your homework and all that." Shannon agreed almost too quickly.

"You guys are a bad influence on me." I gave in, I quickly scribbled my locker combination in her notebook and which books I needed and followed Jerard confidently out of the school.

Jerard lived in a very beautiful white house in New Alden that bore a striking resemblance to a museum. I couldn't imagine how he hadn't gone mad in such a cold feeling house.

"Come on." Jerard jerked his head in the direction of a beautifully carved staircase. I shifted my backpack and followed.

"Oh this is much better." I approved the more contemporary style of the second floor.

"Yeah, they kinda let me have the second floor." Jerard shrugged passing a large very comfy looking sofa in the large, open room at the top of the stairs and moving on down the hallway. At the end of it a door stood ajar.

"Yeah, force of habit." Jerard ushered me into his room. "I don't spend much time out there."

I was happy to see that it wasn't spotlessly clean like I'd often thought he might be. Dirty clothes were strewn across the floor, a bowl sat forgotten on the bedside table and his comforter was in complete disarray.

"I don't really have company over . . ." He added trying to tidy up a bit.

"I don't care, Aiden leaves the house worse than this some days." I shrugged looking around at they keyboard in the corner and the computer desk with a Dell Laptop on it. Jerard settled for straightening the comforter.

"Oh." Jerard dropped his backpack where he stood and retreated into the closet, returning a few minutes later a shirt in his hands. "I can throw that in the washer for you." he motioned to my sauce stained shirt.

"Okay, good luck with that." I nodded taking the shirt from him.

"Oh, I, um, sorry I'll wait outside." Jerard excused himself awkwardly. I laughed to myself as I quickly changed from one shirt to the other and opened the door again. Jerard was leaning against the opposite wall looking completely drained.

"So? Do I look good in your clothes?" I spun around for him.

"You look good in anything." Jerard returned sincerely. Feeling embarrassed I was happy to see the back of him as he disappeared to find the washer.

I busied myself by wandering around his room. The keyboard looked well used, I mad a mental note to ask him to play for me at some point. The desk was cluttered, but I was sure he knew where every thing was. The banana yellow laptop blew my mind. Calm, cool and collected Jerard had an obscenely bright computer. Call me weird if you like, but I think you can tell a lot about someone by their computer – but I didn't know what to make of this. I moved on to his dresser where I found one side occupied by a sports letter laying haphazardly against a snow globe, a music note pinned in the middle of it. I could only guess he had lettered in Band. The other side was dictated by a 5x7 photo of Jerard and his grandfather. James was older, much older than I had ever seen him, but they had the same eyes.

"That was taken two weeks before he died." Jerard appeared over my shoulder.

"It's weird. Seeing him look that frail." I didn't look back at him.

"He was a strong guy, but you could tell the cancer and treatment was getting the better of him by then." Jerard seemed to agree.

"It was cancer that took him?"

"Lung cancer, he had it for ten years. It was pretty bad near the end. Sometimes he knew us, sometimes he didn't. Hell, sometimes he thought I was himself."

"You do look a lot a like." I mentioned.

"That's what everyone always said. After grandpa died, the family kinda went their separate ways."

I turned and watched as he fell to the mattress.

"Nap time?" I smirked sitting next to him. Though the mattress prevented a lot of movement, I could tell he'd nodded. "I'll search for a book to read."

"No. Nap time." Jerard told me in perhaps one of the cutest voices I'd ever heard.

"You want me to nap with you?" I smiled. He nodded. I hesitated.

"I'll be a perfect gentlemen." he promised. "Scout's honor."

"Were you a boy scout?"

"No but you can trust me." He grinned.

I woke up to the sound of my cell phone going off in my bag. It rang once more before declaring that the call had been missed. I rolled onto my back and remembered where I was. To my right, Jerard was still sound asleep with an arm around my waist. I wanted nothing more to curl up and go back to sleep but decided I should check my phone. Missed call: Shannon. I quickly dialed her back.

"Where are you?" she said just loud enough for me to hear her.

"At Jerard's." I told her simply.

"Okay. We're at your house, your mom was asking where you went. Aiden told them you guys were doing homework at the Library." She told me the story.

"Thanks Shan, I'll be back soon. I think." I told her.

"What's going on over there? Why didn't you answer?" Shannon demanded in a less than innocent tone. Behind me Jerard sat bolt up right looking terrified.

"I'll call you back Shan." I shut my flip phone and turned to Jerard. "What's wrong?" Jerard's eyes were out of focus as he jumped out of bed and backed himself towards the wall.

"GET BACK!" He bellowed. "Don't hurt me! I'm James Davenport! U.S. Army! Serial number . . . serial number . . . ." Jerard's voice trailed off, I stared at him rooted on the spot, terrified. He slumped against the wall and slid to a sitting position on the floor. I watched him for a moment, uncertainly and slowly I made my way around the bed.

"Jerard?" I asked softly. Jerard's head lifted and looked up at me, his eyes sliding back into focus.

"Claire? Claire, it is you right?" he looked miserable.

"Yeah," I knelt over him, "It's me, are you okay?"

Jerard leaned up and hugged me to him. Thrown off balance, I fell into him. He refused to let go for a few seconds. Jerard's eyes were heavy, not just from being tired, but they looked emotionally heavy as well.

"Jerard, do you – do you know what happened?" I looked at him properly. He stared back at me looking uncertain.

Jerard pulled into my drive a half an hour later, but we didn't get out. We took a few minutes to collect ourselves before going in the house. It'd been a long few days and it wasn't looking up.

"Are you guys living in the car now?" my window was open and Aiden had come to find us.

"Hey 'Den. No, we're coming in." Jerard cleared his throat opening his door, too indifferent to care that Aiden had punched him the night before.

"Shannon wants you." he nodded towards the porch where Shannon was waiting for us.

"I bet she does." I started towards the house as Aiden stopped Jerard.

"Sorry about last night, man." Aiden shifted uncomfortably. "I got a little crazy." Jerard eyed him (with his good eye) and extended his hand, "Don't worry about it."

"Claire?" Mom asked as we came in the house.

"Its me mom, and Jerard." I told her.

"Is your cell phone broken, young lady?" Mom's hands were on her hips and she looked angry.

"Sorry Mom, I forgot." I shifted uncomfortably.

"Your lucky your brother told us where you were." Mom nodded at Aiden as Shannon stood on the staircase.

"Thanks, Aiden." I tried to say with a straight face.

"And I got a call from school today. You missed a class?" Mom was getting into full swing and I didn't know what to say this time.

"That was my fault, Mrs. Hart." Jerard stepped up. "I kept her late after lunch. If you're tardy they mark you absent." Mom eyed the pair of us. "Try to get her to class on time, Jerard."

"Yes ma'am." Jerard put on his best sorrowful look and Mom went back into the living room.

"Way to think on your feet." Aiden hit Jerard on the shoulder.

"Shush Aiden!" Shannon hissed jerking her head in the direction of the living room. We all leaned to look into the living room, Mom and Landon were wrapped up in the nightly news.

"No harm, no foul." Aiden stuck his tongue out at Shannon.

"You are so immature." Shannon rolled her eyes, "Come on, Claire, girl time."

"Consider yourself banished." I put my hand on Jerard's shoulder.

"Video games?" Aiden offered, Jerard shrugged and followed him up the stairs taking a moment to glance back at me as they left. I sighed to myself and followed Shannon to my room.

"What's up?" I shut the door behind us. Shannon held up a hand while she dialed her phone with the other. I dropped my backpack in the middle of the floor and fell onto my bed. Shannon clicked on her speaker phone and sat next to me.

"Hey Shannon," Ana's voice rung out, "What's up?"

"Claire finally came home." Shannon grinned at me.

"Hi Ana." I chimed.

"It's about time! Where have you been?" Ana practically screamed.

"Mom?" I tilted my head at Shannon.

"Yeah, yeah, spill it girl." Ana ignored my jab at her, as Shannon laughed. So I told Ana and Shannon about everything that had happened that day: the nap and the project we were doing giving as few details as I could about the latter. It didn't matter, after they heard that Jerard and I were napping together nothing school related mattered at all.

THURSDAY

"I HAVE A week worth of detention because of you." Persephone yanked me around at school the next morning as I walked with Ryan.

"Hey!" Ryan snapped at her.

Persephone ignored him, "You're going to pay for this."

"Oh yeah, I made you throw that tray at me." I replied sarcastically. "Get over yourself already." Ryan and I turned to leave.

"This isn't a game. I'm missing a lot of appointments this week!" she stamped her foot in agitation.

"Listen princess. I don't care if you don't get your hair bleached or your manicure this week. You were stupid, not my problem." I turned on her.

"I don't bleach my hair!" She gasped.

"Oh, right, blondes always have black roots. My bad." I rolled my eyes and walked off with Ryan.

Things were mostly back to normal with in the group today. Ryan and Key admitted to knowing Aiden, and Shannon was no longer between a rock and a hard place. All that was left was getting through the next two days with out doing major bodily harm to myself or anyone else.

Things were getting screwed up on so many levels though. My morning classes seemed to be nothing but a fog of disconnected words, all I could do was hope that they came around when I'd have to do my homework that night. Moving to Alden's Hollow had been an adventure, and honestly a lot better than I had ever planned, but I was getting tired of drama. If this was a prelude to what the rest of the year was going to be like transferring back to Oakdale wouldn't be so horrible.

"Deep in thought again?" Key caught up with me outside of Journalism.

"What? Oh, hey Key." I greeted him, "Yeah."

"You seem heavy hearted lately." Key observed as we made our way towards the lunch room.

"Lots of drama going on."

"Oh yeah, good job at getting Persephone thrown in detention." he nudged me playfully.

I laughed, "I wish I could take credit for that one, from what I hear Mrs. Lancaster was supposed to be where Mrs. Harper was. If Lancaster had been there I'm sure she would have gotten away with it."

"Yeah, Ryan held her up at the end of his history class." Key grinned mischievously.

"You knew about that?" I grinned back.

"We might have heard that something was going to happen at lunch, and that Mrs. Lancaster was going to look the other way." He winked.

"You guys are amazing." I shook my head laughing, Key wrapped and arm around my neck.

"It's about time someone got her."

Lunch was a fairly lighthearted affair with Shannon filling us in on all the last minute party details and giving us our pre-party duties no one really got a word in edgewise.

As we came around the corner on our way to History that day, Mrs. Lancaster was standing in her usual spot outside her door. I couldn't help thinking she was the sort of teacher who wanted to be in the middle of the action should something happen. I sighed heavily, and Jerard's hand found mine giving it an encouraging squeeze as we headed into the battle zone.

"Mr. Lane, Miss. Weston." She folded her arms.

"Mrs. Lancaster." We chimed attempting to go into the classroom, but she stood in the doorway.

"You were absent yesterday."

"Yep." I nodded, not sure where she was going with this.

"Where were you?" she demanded to know.

"At home." Jerard answered. It was true, he was at home, she didn't need to know that I wasn't actually at my home.

"Maybe I should call your parents and confirm that. Such young and intelligent minds shouldn't be wasting their education." she raised a brow.

"Feel free." I called her bluff.

"Good luck. My parents are on a dig. If you can get a hold of them, tell them I say hi." Jerard went on. If looks could kill, Jerard and I would have died as we ducked under her arm just before the bell rang.

"She's going to have it out for us for the rest of the year." I mentioned to Jerard as we took our seats and opened our books.

"Probably." Jerard shrugged. "Think you can handle it?" I smirked at him as she called our attention.

"Attention everyone!" The class fell reluctantly silent.

"Ah, thank you. I'm sure you're projects are coming along quite well. Remember they are due first thing Monday afternoon! That being said, I suggest some of you make a trip to the Alden's Hollow Historical Society this weekend. Nina and Sarah, there is a lot of information on the Lumberyard fire there. Hannah and Michael – if you speak to Tessa Jones I'm sure she'll have plenty of information for you on the group of young men who served in World War II from the area. And Claire and Jerard. I'd like you in particular to go talk to Curtis Mitchell, he'll have an interesting spin on Fiona Kelly's disappearance for you." Mrs. Lancaster lingered on us.

There was no way anyone else could have missed the bit of fire that seemed to raise in her eyes, but our fellow classmates went on as if the devil herself wasn't in the room with us. Behind me Jerard snorted as Mrs. Lancaster told us to open our books to page forty-nine.

"What?" I muttered to him.

"I bet we have a more interesting spin on the project than he does." I forced a laugh, knowing exactly what he meant.

When we were released from our personal hell for the day Jerard and I decided to take a trip to the historical society anyway. Not really knowing where else to go in our search for Aunt Ona.

The Historical Society was in the heart of Old Town. In what was once the town hall. It was old, and musty and you could even see where pieces of wood had deteriorated over the years. I looked around wondering if we were wandering into a death trap just stepping foot over the threshold.

"Don't worry Miss," I jumped at a male voice as I examined a particularly bad looking spot, "It's perfectly safe here. We've replaced a good amount of the original structure, but left in a few pieces for a bit of old world finesse. Quite charming, don't you think?" The man striding toward us had gray hair and a crew cut, a rounder build, and when he smiled, it didn't exactly meet his eyes.

"Uh, sure." I looked at Jerard.

"What can I do for you today?" he went on, "I'm Curtis Mitchell, by the way, at your service."

"Uh," Jerard looked him over, "I'm Jerard, this is Claire. We heard you could tell us about Fiona Kelly?"

"Ah yes, we've had a lot of people come in to inquire about that. With the anniversary coming up." he nodded thoughtfully, "Right this way. I'm something of a Kelly expert if you will." Curtis led the way down a small hallway and into a dimly lit room. *A Kelly expert? Who the hell does this guy think he's fooling?*

"What's your interest in Fiona Kelly, if I may ask?" Curtis moved towards a corner on the far side of the room.

"We're doing a project on her." Jerard replied, I was content to listen having the feeling that there was a good chance that I would tell this guy off if I opened my mouth. There was something about him that I just didn't like.

"Ah, you must be from Dana Lancaster's class. You've come to the right place then. She's something of a local hero here." Curtis motioned to the photos. There were a few baby photos of her in a bonnet and hugging a teddy bear, a few grade school ones showing many gap tooth smiles, even one of her modeling her wedding gown. I didn't realize it at first but after a second glance at that particular photo, I recognized the little girl holding up her train to be my very own mother. It took me a moment to recover from that, but then the last photo was Fiona in the woods somewhere near a large open rock face. The night at the Cliffs came back to me.

"Where's this?" I pointed to the photo, cutting off Curtis mid-sentence.

"Out near the cliffs. It's supposed to be closed now." Curtis replied, "All the kids used to go to that cave."

"What can you tell us," Jerard went on, "About her and James Davenport?"

"Ah, yes." Curtis looked like he's been offered a brand new car. "He is a fascinating subject in himself. Well as most know, they were quite the couple. Named most handsome couple of Alden Senior High James's senior year. She adored him, Fiona did. Though the story isn't as clean cut as those fools at the Alden Daily Bugle reported it to be."

"What do you mean?" I demanded sharply. Curtis glanced at me before his lips curled into what he must have thought was a charming smile, but instead it was a nasty grin.

"Well, my dear," He emphasized the last two words, "It's true when he was in Korea he proposed to Fiona via mail. That's not to say that he was a . . . good boy there. He was quite the fraternizer, if you catch my drift."

"He was a womanizer?" Jerard's eyes narrowed.

"To say the least. But what else is to be expected, I mean being on the front lines, never knowing when you could be killed. You have to remember that in those days men ruled the way things went. Women had no say." Curtis glanced at me, despite my fascination with the photo I'd seen I narrowed my eyes at him. *I bet you'd like it to* still *be that way, you scumbag.*

"So what does this have to do with him and Fiona?" I growled, "He still loved Fiona, no matter what he did on the front line he was still coming home to her. They were still getting married."

"It's more to the point that people have a glossed over version of James Davenport. You know war hero, romantic, faithful. We have written testimonies," He waved to a near by case, "from his trench buddies. The stories they could and did tell about squeaky clean James Davenport."

"What about Charlie Fiske?" Jerard chimed in, he looked slightly scandalized. "He was his best friend and never said anything against him."

"*He* is the true hero." Curtis' tone changed dramatically. "Did you know he was a prisoner of war? When they finally released him back to our side he weighed no more than a hundred pounds and had cuts all over his body. James Davenport only looked like the epitome of apple pie and the red, white and blue. The things he saw, the things he *did*. Would make any normal man blush." Curtis went on.

"How do you know this?" I glared at him, "You act like you were there."

"As a matter of fact miss," he puffed out what was left of his chest, "I was. Lieutenant Colonel Curtis R. Mitchell, United States Army, retired."

You could have heard a pin drop miles from where we stood. Jerard looked like he was hit with a brick, his mouth working furiously but not a sound or a word escaped his lips. Curtis, I noticed upon his revelation, did stand straighter than a normal person would, and his shoes were shined expertly. How could we have been so dumb? After a moment, Jerard finally broke his silence.

"Were you in his unit?"

"Only for a few weeks, before he was sent home with that wound." Curtis looked irritated. I was willing to bet that he had never received a purple heart. Jerard glanced at me.

"What about Fiona?" I interjected before his bitterness could get anymore apparent.

"What about her?" Curtis snapped.

"Well. That's who we're supposed to do the report on." I told him plainly. "Have there been any reports about what happened to her the day she disappeared? Where she was going? Who she was with?" Curtis lingered on a glare directed at Jerard, who looked mutinous, before answering my question.

"She was with her mother in the morning, finishing up wedding details that ended up going on into the afternoon. They had supper around five o'clock and about seven she went out to Alden City Park with Davenport and Fiske. Fiske says that they left the park around eight thirty to go work on his car. He said that Fiona was still sitting out on The Cliffs when they left. She never came home." he explained. Something didn't sound right about that explanation, though I couldn't put my finger exactly on why.

"What was Charlie doing there?" I asked.

"Fiske was going to be Davenport's best man, the three of them were always seen together. Thick as thieves, they were." Curtis went on, "Though Fiske was more like a faithful dog than a friend. He was always seen catering to whatever Davenport wanted. It was kind of sickening, really to demote himself to such a level after all he'd been through."

Jerard made to move towards Curtis, I quickly grabbed his hand to restrain him a little. He seemed to catch himself and made it look like he'd tripped over his own feet.

"Thanks for you're time, Mr. Mitchell." I squeezed Jerard's hand. "We'll show ourselves out." with that I pulled Jerard towards the front of the building. I could feel the anger radiating off of him as we went through the door out onto the street. It was pouring now, I hoped the cool water would cool him down as well.

"Can you believe that guy?" He exclaimed gesturing to the doorway, with a not-so-nice hand gesture. "I mean, my grandpa was a good man. How can he spread all those rumors about him?" I put my hand on his arm.

"Jerard, stop and breathe, please?" Jerard looked down at me, the rain flattening his shaggy hair to his head. He took a deep breath and let it out.

"Sorry." he apologized.

"Don't be. But . . ." I hesitated for a minute, "Are you sure those things couldn't be true?"

Jerard gave me an angry look, "You don't actually believe him do you?"

"All I'm saying is war changes people." I bit my lip. "You're grandpa may have been a good man. But who says the trauma of war didn't make him end up that way?"

Jerard stared at me.

"Think about it Jerard, think about what we seen." I reminded him of our latest 'vision.' "Charlie and your grandpa had been fighting."

"We don't know what about though." he answered seeming a bit desperate to hold on to his grandpa's good memory.

"I know." I squeezed his hand, "I know."

Jerard's driving made me a bit nervous with the stony eyed look he kept, but he stayed between the lines perfectly. Whether he'd purposely gone to the cliffs, or if we were simply being drawn beyond our control to that spot, we found ourselves making our way over the rocks again. I was slipping on the wet stone but kept up pretty well.

"It's pretty here," I commented as he helped me up onto a particularly large rock, hoping to get his mind off of his anger. "do a lot of people come out here?"

"Yeah, a lot of kids at school go cliff jumping over there." Jerard pointed to a ridge that looked quite perilous.

"Why?" I jumped down from my perch. Just being accident prone, I suddenly found myself flat on my butt on a rock after landing wrong.

"How did you make it to seventeen?" Jerard laughed helping me up.

"A fluke I bet." I massaged my butt a little hoping the stinging would stop. He grinned at me as I gingerly made my way over to the edge he'd pointed to.

"Why would anyone jump off this?"

"Thrill seekers. It's pretty cool." he said not looking at.

"*You've* done it?"

"Yeah, a couple times." he grinned at me.

"You're crazy." I didn't realize just how crazy he was until we got to the side and I looked down. I wasn't a great swimmer, I'm sure I would have panicked if I had ever jumped and most likely drown. But being the masochist I am, I leaned over the edge slightly to get a better look.

"You *can* take a step back Claire, your as white as a ghost." Jerard reminded me.

I would have loved to take his advice. But the problem was apparently it wasn't in the cards. I felt a strong bit of pressure between my shoulder blades and I was sent hurling forward over the edge. Everything seemed to move in slow motion. I could see Jerard standing near the edge, frozen, watching me fall into the lake. When he disappeared I could see the crevices and protruding bits of rock in the face of the cliff. Had I not been so terrified I'm pretty sure I would have found this incredibly exciting.

But I felt instead of saw, the second I hit the water, I was trying desperately to make my way to the surface but every inch of me seemed to constrict. Every now and then I could feel my lungs re-expand and I vaguely felt someone in the water with me. My eyes slid back, and it was like I was outside of my body. I hovered a few feet above the water, watching Jerard trying furiously to get my limp body to shore. I followed slowly behind intrigued by this new feeling. The feeling of weightlessness, and a care free heart. Jerard was now in knee deep water carrying me onto the small beach that I could only assume was where the cliff jumpers came out. If the new feelings I had weren't so great I would have felt sorry for the worried look on Jerard's usually happy face.

"You'll live." I heard a voice say. I spun quickly to find Aunt Fiona hovering just behind me. "He pushed you, Claire." She came closer to me and smiled. "You look so much like Amelia."

"A-Aunt Fiona?"

"Yes," she nodded, "I needed to talk to you, but I'm not nearly strong enough to show myself to you in another way."

"Am I dead?" I looked at Jerard, who was now performing CPR on me.

"Yes," she nodded, "But you'll live. I promise you that. I don't have much time Claire, you must listen. Find my body. I can't leave this realm with out someone finding me."

"Where is it?" I asked not able to tear my eyes from Jerard, he was saying words to my body that I couldn't hear.

"I can't tell you. You're not alone though, he's helping too. James is, we brought you two together." Fiona shook her head, "But you must be careful. The man they said killed me, Mr. Taylor, he's going to try to work against you. He's a very angry man, he tried to commit the murder he was imprisoned for, he sensed my blood in you. Look after him," she motioned to Jerard, "The man thinks he is James." I started to feel something tug at my heart.

"Why can't you tell me?"

"I am bound by death. I know you can do it, Claire. Find me, please." Aunt Fiona's voice was starting to sound distant. "Tell Amelia, tell her that I don't blame her for the dress." It was like being sucked into outer space, I felt myself rushing back to my body.

"Claire! Come on, Claire! You have to live!" Jerard's voice was the distant one now. I felt the water in my lungs loosen. His hands pumped my chest and I felt him breathe air into me, the water was moving towards my throat. His voice sounded terrified, and I felt concern again for the first time. *I'm going to live. Aunt Fiona said I was going to live. Don't give up Jerard! Please don't give up . . . save me like James never saved Fiona . . .* I coughed and sputtered as water came out of my mouth, onto the beach.

"Claire?" his voice sounded tired and scared. I could barely open my eyes as he sat me up. My eyes may have refused to open all the way, but I didn't need them to tell that those beautiful blue eyes we wrought with concern.

"I'm sorry." I croaked, and immediately wished I hadn't. My throat was searing with pain, I tried to lift my hand to my throat but I couldn't. I felt weak and tired.

"Don't say that it wasn't your fault." He took my face in his hands. "I shouldn't have brought you here again. I don't understand one minute you were there and then the next you were . . ." he stopped himself not wanting to relive it. I shook my head and I could have swore that my brain sloshed around a little bit inside. I must have started to sway a little because he suddenly grasped my arms. "Can you walk? Do you want to go to the hospital?"

"No!" I yelped, tears came to my eyes as my throat throbbed. He jumped at my abrupt reaction.

"Home?" I shook my head again, trying not to think about having to explain to what happened to Mom and Landon. Mom would go insane and send me straight to the doctor. No, this was too much for her.

"I'll take you to my house then, you can't be alone right now." Jerard decided after a minute. "Come on, I'll help you." Jerard helped me up slowly, trying his best not to disorient me anymore than I already was. I didn't really remember how we got back to the Liberty, I was too out of it. When we arrived back at Jerard's house I nearly fell out of the Jeep.

"Are you still with me, Claire?" His voice sounded distant again, and I wondered if it was just because I was tired, or if I was going to lose consciousness again. I fought to keep my eyes open and groaned to let him know I was listening. My throat responded angrily and I winced. Before I realized it, we were in what had to be his room. He sat me down in a computer chair and shuffled through his dresser, returning to me with a pair of pajama pants and a t shirt.

"Here, put these on." with that he left the room and closed the door. It took a moment for me to register that he'd actually gone. When it did though I started to feel scared at the idea of it. As quickly as my useless limbs would allow me I changed into the warm, dry clothes he'd given me and stumbled towards the door, yanking it open. When I saw his face, I started to calm down a little. He looked down at me, taking the wet clothes from my hands.

"Lie down, get under the covers. I'll be right back." He told me, his free hand brushing my damp bangs out of my face. I wanted to protest, but I just didn't have it in me. I wandered aimlessly back into the room, noticing that his room was neater than the last time I'd been there, and thanking my good graces that it was. Once I was under his warm blankets, it was too difficult to fight the exhaustion taking over me. I don't even remember Jerard returning to me. For that I was sad, but he was there when I woke up. I was warm, but felt like I was hit by a truck. I cringed as I turned over, apparently I'd hit the water hard.

"Hey," he murmured brushing his fingers against my cheek, "I thought you'd be out longer than this."

"How . . . long . . . ?" I gasped, it hadn't gotten any better and I whimpered a little.

"Shh." he stared down at me. "Don't hurt yourself, I've been watching over you for the last hour and a half." I nodded slowly, on the bedside table Jerard's phone went off.

"Hey Aiden." He greeted, "I-I don't know, I'll ask her." Jerard covered the mouth piece and looked at me. "They're going to The Barrel for dinner, Shannon and the rest. Think you'd be up to it?"

"I can do it." I said slowly trying not to irritate my vocal chords.

"Okay, yeah we'll be there." Jerard told my stepbrother. "See you in a bit."

"Are you sure you're okay for this?" Jerard closed his phone.

"I'll be fine. Where are my clothes?" I whispered, whispering was better than talking right now.

"I'll get them." He nodded, I looked down at the oversized clothes and thought that I seemed to be wearing his clothes more than my own these days. I got up slowly, every inch of my body hurt and waited for him to return.

We got to the Barrel around six o'clock and found Aiden and the rest at a large table near the back. It wasn't long before we were all sharing pizza and pitchers of pop. For the second time today, I felt outside of my body, Jerard looked as if he felt the same. No one commented on my slightly disheveled appearance, but were too wrapped up in the pool party, the football game Friday and the festival on Saturday to really care if I was wearing make up anymore. Ana tried to engage me in conversation about this her boy-toy Declan, but I just wasn't interested. The idea of such a trivial thing as a crush was of little importance to me.

My aunt was in fact dead, and I didn't even have chance to tell Jerard yet. That was a key part to our project, not that I could really look at it as a project anymore. Not just that, but Richard Taylor really had been innocent. I hated Mrs. Lancaster but I felt bad that she grew up with out a father when it could have been avoided. I had no idea how we were going to bring it all together. I didn't know where our next break would come from but something needed to point us in the right direction soon.

I watched my friends happy faces with out really hearing them. Shannon held on to Aiden's arm so lovingly, and Key despite the negative influence I knew he was getting at home still spoke so animatedly. Ryan, his partner in crime hanging on his every word waiting to get a good joke in edgewise. It was fun to watch those two play off of each other. Ana chimed in with Shannon on pop culture and always seemed to have something to counter her overly dreamy comments. As I stared around at them, I wondered what Jerard and I must have looked like. Two severely melancholy teenagers? The distant ones? I didn't know, but what I did know was at that moment there was a real line that divided us from our friends. They worried about boys and tests, I worried about whether or not I'd actually live to see Friday and Jerard . . . well I guessed he wondered if he was going crazy with all the weird things that had been happening.

After dinner we walked through Old Town to Icy Sweets. The early September breeze made me wonder why we were getting ice cream but the idea of being out with my friends rather than going home to deal with homework and parents was by far better. Jerard held my hand, constantly glancing at me to make sure I was okay. I appreciated his concern, but after a while it looked as if he'd developed a nervous twitch.

"Come on, Claire!" Shannon dragged me away from Jerard to walk with her and Ana.

"Hi guys." I replied quietly.

"What's up with you guys, you and Jerard?" Ana went on. "You both looked like zombies during dinner."

I wasn't sure if I really wanted to let Shannon and Ana in on it, but I swore them to secrecy. Which meant I knew Shannon would tell Aiden at some point, but I wasn't too concerned about him, and told them everything that had happened at the lake, minus the out of body experience. How Jerard had saved my life, how he'd taken care of me, and the creepy feelings we got out at the Cliffs now. They listened in sort of awe, never interrupting me. When I finally finished my story they looked at me with concerned eyes.

"Are you okay? Do you need to go to the hospital?" Shannon looked me over more closely now.

"I'm fine, my throat hurts and my chest, but that's it." I shook my head. "You guys can't tell Mom or Landon, promise me."

"I promise." They chimed lowly.

"Claire! You could have died!" Ana pointed out needlessly, "He saved your life."

"I know!" I looked around to make sure the boys weren't listening.

"Is that why you guys have been off on your own so much?" Shannon went on. "The history thing?" I nodded.

At home, Aiden went straight into the house leaving us on the porch alone. He looked at me and shifted uncomfortably.

"Fiona's dead isn't she?"

I nodded silently.

"Did my grandpa have something to do with it?"

"I don't know."

"You said something to me out there tonight." he went on.

"What did I say?"

"You asked me to save you . . . like my grandfather never saved Fiona." he looked uncertain.

"I don't know what made me say that, but if your grandpa was there and didn't help it was for a really good reason. He loved her." I tried to back track. Deep down I knew that James had been with my aunt the night she died, but I couldn't prove it. Nor did I know if he let her die.

"I know he did. I can feel it." he muttered.

Jerard left looking like he felt uncomfortable, and understandably so, I mean I pretty much put him on the spot unknowingly with what I said about his grandpa.

"Claire, Key's downstairs." Sam stood in my doorway a little while later.

"Key?" I glanced at my clock. "It's almost nine o'clock. What's he want?"

Sam shrugged. "I don't know. He's waiting for you on the porch."

" . . . Okay." I set my biology book aside and made my way downstairs.

Key stood with his back to the door, his long hair damp and loose, his hands shoved into his pockets. He was looking out over our neighborhood and though I couldn't see his face I had the feeling that he was doing some heavy thinking as well. I stepped out onto the porch, shutting the door quietly behind me.

"Key?" I touched his shoulder, "Is everything okay?" Key turned his head to the side looking down at me.

"I could ask you the same thing."

"I . . . what?" I tilted my head at him.

"Come for a walk with me." Key offered motioning to the sidewalk.

"I dunno Key, it's getting kinda late. Mom might freak." I glanced back at the door.

"Just around the block?" he suggested.

I couldn't see that taking too long so I agreed and followed him down the steps. The first minute or so was lost in silence.

"You shouldn't tell Shannon things." Key said suddenly. "You know she can't keep a secret."

"Ah, so that's what this is about." I smiled at him, "I should have expected that."

"Yeah, you should have." he nodded slowly, "So, are you okay?"

"I hurt," I looped my arm in his, "but still living. Jerard took pretty good care of me."

"I thought you guys were off at dinner." Key said, "Does any one else know?"

"You mean other than the rest of the school?" I grinned at him, "If you know, I'm gathering the whole group knows. But if anyone tells Mom and Landon I'll personally beat them senseless."

"Good point." He laughed.

"How are you doing? You seemed pretty thought consumed." I went on.

"Okay." he replied elusively.

"That sounds very . . . satisfactory." I raised a brow at him. "Your dad still on your case?"

"Him and Grandfather." his voice was monotone. "Grades and all that."

"You make good grades don't you?" I tiled my head at him as we rounded the first corner.

"Fair." he shrugged, "I wouldn't care as much if they weren't tearing me in different directions."

"What do you mean?"

"Dad says I won't amount to anything. Grandfather though, he says I should make my tribe proud and make something of myself."

"You should listen to your grandfather." I mentioned conversationally.

"Yeah. But I live with dad." he smirked.

FRIDAY

FIONA WAS LAUGHING almost lyrically as she skipped through the woods.

"James! Come on!" she called her long red hair falling across her face as she turned to look back at him. James was casually walking along behind her, a pleasant smile playing at his lips. As if he were enjoying her carefree will. It hadn't been tarnished by the ravages of war. She twirled around, her skirt flowing around her as she faced forward again. She looked like an angel. James's angel, she was put on this earth for him. Fiona led the way to the cave, everyone went there but it was their special place. James turned on his flashlight and followed lighting the way along the path Fiona knew so well. She'd traveled it more times than she could remember while he was away. It reminded her of him. They didn't stay on the main path, but took a side fork to the left. The cavern they entered was smaller than the one they'd just left but it was in an odd way . . . cozy. They were caught up in their own little world, nothing, not even the cold inside the dark damp cave could touch them.

My cell phone rang at three o'clock in the morning. It took me a moment to wake up and look at the caller ID.

"Jerard?" I turned over.

"Hey." his voice was quiet and uncertain.

"What's wrong, love?"

"I had another nightmare. My grandpa killed a man with his bare hands." he told me softly.

"He . . . what?" I tried to make heads or tails of his statement.

"They were crossing a river, and they were ambushed. Gun shots were going off everywhere but my Grandpa's gun jammed. He drowned a man Claire. I saw it."

"Wow." I replied waking up a bit more.

"I woke up just as the North Korean died." He went on, "It freaked me out. I'm tired of all the death. I'm tired of being alone."

"I'll ask Landon if you can come stay with us for a few days if you'd like?" I suggested. "I doubt he'd mind."

"Yeah, would you please?" He agreed slowly.

"Sure. Are you going to be okay?" I went on.

"Yeah, I just wanted to hear your voice is all. I'll see you in a few hours." Jerard answered convincingly.

"Okay. Goodnight . . ."

"Goodnight, Claire."

I woke up with my chest hurting and a head aching, being able to focus on it now. Downstairs I heard Mom yell for me to get out of bed and then Sam and Aiden. I stared up at the ceiling trying to decide whether or not Mom would buy me being sick.

"Claire-Fiona-Kelly-Weston!" Mom punctuated each name as much as possible as she yelled up the stairs.

"Okay! I'm getting up!" I screamed back, my chest feeling like it was going to explode from the throat down. I was towel drying my hair when I noticed Aiden leaning against the door frame his arms folded across his chest.

"Hi."

"Hey." he replied simply. I dropped the towel on the floor and grabbed my brush feeling a little awkward.

"What can I do for you?"

"I talked to Jer late last night." I froze for a moment. "Oh?"

"He told me what happened at the lake." I saw him glance over his shoulder into the hallway. "Are you okay?"

"Um, sure. It hurts to talk and my chest is a little heavy, but its fine." I bit my lip.

"You better get moving. Mom's on the verge of throwing a fit." Aiden straightened up.

"Okay." I smiled noting that he called my Mom, 'mom' too.

"You can have Jerard, but if you start dating any of my other friends, you'll have to clear it with me first. I know how some of those guys talk." he told me, "You're not wearing that, are you?" I looked down at my typical jeans and t-shirt in question.

"What's wrong with this?" I asked finding it amusing that I was about to hear fashion advice from Aiden and his quickness to change the subject. Not that I wasn't thankful for the latter.

"You have to wear green and yellow" Aiden stated plainly.

"Why?" I shouldered my messenger bag, checking it for all my books.

"The pep rally. School spirit, Claire, school spirit!" Aiden shook his head pointing to his own ASH Wrestling t-shirt.

"There's a pep rally today?" I asked absently following him down the stairs.

"First football game of the year, they always hold a pep rally. They throw in some back to school stuff too but its mostly about the game." Aiden clued me in, "Its during sixth hour."

"At least we'll get away from Mrs. Lancaster." I muttered darkly. "Hey, Aiden, I need you to do me a favor."

"Depends?"

"Jerard wants to get away from his house for a night or two, do you think you can ask Landon if he can stay here?"

"Oh yeah, sure. Just keep the making out to a minimum." he looked a little unnerved by the idea.

"Yeah, yeah."

"You okay? Outside of what happened last night?" Aiden held me back at the bottom of the stairs. "You and Jer have been acting weird lately, even for you guys."

"We're a bit preoccupied." I ran my hand through my hair.

"What's up?" Without preamble, I spilled the whole story to Aiden, and inadvertently Sam who appeared on the stairs in front of us, leaving nothing out.

"And now, Jerard and I are both kinda numb for the brain down." I sighed as I finished the story.

Aiden leaned sideways against the wall on the other side of the stairs and let out a low whistle.

"That's intense."

"I can do some research on Paranormal activity for you Claire, and ways to contact the dead. We could even try to get an exorcism done. But that has to be sanctioned by the church and that could take some time . . . I'll see what I can find." Sam went on jabbering as we walked into the kitchen. I stared after him praying he had the good sense to stop before Mom and Landon heard anything.

"I don't know what to do, Aiden." I went on, "Jerard's not sleeping, I'm confused as hell, meanwhile there are supernatural forces at work that *no one* can understand. Once upon a time high school was supposed to be about dances and who was dating who. Not a Scooby Doo mystery."

"So that's why Jer wants to stay with us?" I nodded.

"You two are talking civilly?" Jerard came through the front door.

"God is having a good day." I shrugged following Aiden into the kitchen.

"Morning kids!" Landon boomed flipping a pancake high up in to the air and letting it land on the griddle.

"Nice catch, Landon." Jerard nodded approvingly.

"Hungry?" Landon grinned at him as I grabbed a peach from the fruit bowl.

"No, thanks." Jerard laughed as Aiden tore into a stack of his own.

"Dad, Claire doesn't have any ASH stuff." Aiden pointed out through a mouthful of pancake and syrup. "Today's the pep rally."

"Oh! Yeah we have to do something about that." Landon agreed, he reached into his wallet and handed me a fifty-dollar bill.

"I – this really isn't – its not that big of a deal." I stared at the bill in my hand.

"Make sure she gets a shirt or something this morning." Landon winked at Jerard. Jerard plucked the bill out of my hand.

"I got it covered. I'll buy one for her if it comes to it." Jerard stuffed the bill in his own pocket.

"Thanks, Jer. Are you ready to go? Or would you and Dad like to find something else to conspire together on?" I raised a brow at him.

"Sure. See you at school 'Den." Jerard smiled, I rolled my eyes dropping the peach into my lunch bag and following him out to the Jeep.

"You ready to show some school spirit?" Jerard grinned at me, in his overly sarcastic joking tone.

"I don't see you in school apparel." I pointed out to him. Jerard twisted in the driver seat and unbuttoned his checked over shirt to reveal a white ASH t-shirt. "You suck."

"Don't worry, at least you're not a cheerleader." Jerard tried to cheer me up.

"Thank god." I muttered. "If you're done playing Johnny Football I'll tell you about the dream I had last night." Jerard snickered but sobered up enough to listen to my dream about Fiona and James.

"I think she's getting desperate, like we're taking too long. But she doesn't know how to help us anymore. Have you ever seen this cave?" I finished just as we were turning into the student lot. He looked thoughtful as we searched for a parking spot.

"I think so." he replied after a moment as we pulled into a parking space. "We'll go after school."

I was so glad that in a few short hours I'd be free for the weekend. Though I use the term "free" loosely. I hoped that the party tonight, and the festival tomorrow would take my mind off of all the loose ends on Aunt Ona's mystery, but we were no closer to even starting our paper on it. Sunday night was going to be a long night, I could see it already.

But I still had to get through the next few days before I had to worry about that. Meanwhile we ran into Ryan and Key before we headed, reluctantly on my end, to the school store.

"Good morning, my lady." Ryan kissed my hand.

"New ploy to get women?" I asked, "Trying chivalry?"

"Sexual harassment isn't getting him anywhere." Key retorted.

"I can't imagine why." I grinned at him.

"What're you guys up to?" Key went on.

"Lady Claire," Jerard winked at me, "has to be initiated into ASH. Landon wants us to get her a hoodie or something for the pep rally."

"Ah, is that all we're doing for her?" Ryan followed us down the hallway. "We're not going to make her knock over a gas station or something?"

"She's cute enough, she'd get away with it." Key shrugged.

"I love how you guys always talk about me like I wasn't here." I glanced around at the three of them.

"It's 'cause your short." Jerard answered, I glared at him playfully.

"Shannon's going crazy." Ryan went on, "I've gotten three texts from her already this morning."

"What's the matter with her?" I looked up at him.

"Party stuff, she needs us to go to Wal-Mart to get napkins and all that stuff. Her dad forgot them last night."

"She's freaking out over napkins?" I raised a brow.

"Well, you have to know Shannon. She kinda views this second only to prom." Jerard explained to me.

"Yeah . . ." I replied as we walked into the lobby. "Yeah, I could see that."

"She's going to be like Hitler at lunch today. She always has a check list before these things." Key went on as he held the door open to the Pro Shop.

"Aren't pro shops in skating rinks?" I mentioned as passed him.

"Yeah, but they figure since this is where you get your varsity jackets and blankets and all things Alden Senior High, it's the Pro Shop." Ryan shrugged.

"How about this?" Jerard held up a hot pink t-shirt, as Ryan and Key went off in search of early morning sugar.

"That's not green or yellow." I wrinkled my nose at it.

"Okay green or yellow?" he gave me the option.

"Green."

"Good, I like green on you." he moved over to a rack with green shirts and hoodies on it.

"Hoodie or t-shirt?" he went on.

"Hoodie." Jerard picked out a simple green hoodie with "Alden Senior High" written across the chest in block lettering and tossed it to me. "Perfect. But you got the money." I checked the size before I tossed it back to him.

"Oh yeah." he smiled grabbing the bill from his pocket and brought the hoodie to the counter. "Hey Mr. Williams, just this, please." he put the hoodie on the counter.

"Hello Mr. Lane, you know, you should really think about flowers instead." He nodded in my direction. I laughed openly.

"The quickest way to a girl's heart is keeping her warm, didn't they teach you that?" Jerard grinned at me.

"I'm not up on the new advances, Jerard, we still held hands, I hear we're up to shameless groping now." Mr. Williams scanned the hoodie through.

"That's the Ryan Winters approach." Jerard said loudly.

Ryan looked up from the candy rack. "What?"

"Ah, yes, I've heard that." Mr. Williams surveyed Ryan.

"What?" he repeated.

"Nothing, nothing." Mr. Williams shook his head, sneaking a wink to Jerard and I as we paid.

"Don't worry sir," I patted Jerard on the shoulder, "He's an old soul. I haven't been groped."

"Good for you, boy." Mr. Williams nodded giving me the hoodie

"Thanks." we chorused and left the store. Just outside the door Jerard took my bag and made me put on my new hoodie.

"Happy now?" I spread my arms to him.

"Yep, you look good." He nodded as he gave me my bag back.

"Thanks." I laughed as Ryan and Key joined us.

"So what's this pep rally?" I asked, "Do we have to go?"

"Oh its back to school stuff. Mr. Bishop pretends to get us excited for the school year while every just kind zones out to their cell phones." Ryan shrugged. "But yeah, it is mandatory."

"Well at least it gets us out of Lancaster's class." I sighed.

"Hey, we're going over to the courtyard, there's still time for a game of hackey sack before school." Ryan told us a few moments later at my locker.

"Go for the gold, guys." I put away my math book and grabbed my English and Science books. Jerard laughed as I slammed my locker shut and they took off. Jerard looked down at me as we were left to ourselves.

"Are you okay? Did you ever get back to sleep?" I leaned against my locker.

"On and off." he shrugged.

"Aiden's going to ask Landon if you can stay." I told him. Jerard nodded, I reached up and pressed some of his dark hair back behind his ear. "It'll be okay."

"I know. I'm with you." Jerard placed his hand on the back my neck. "So far, so good." he smiled, "Grandpa if you ruin this for me I swear . . ." Jerard never finished his threat, he was too busy kissing me.

"Ow ow!" Key's voice sounded in my ears.

"Well, it wasn't your grandpa." I laughed quietly as we broke apart. "I thought you were playing hackey sack?"

"Man, you get all the girls." Ryan ignored me. "Well, with him off the market, maybe a few will settle for us now."

"Pass, women are nothing but trouble."

The bell rang a few minutes later and our group went their separate ways. My classes were still blurring, though the only good part about that is they seemed to go by faster that way. Before I knew it math had finished and Jerard and I were heading out into the hallway. We seemed to be exempt from the two-more-hours-until-freedom rowdiness as we dodged two cheerleaders and a football.

I wasn't particularly interested in the school spirit aspect of today, but at least it was a change from the drones that had been walking around school the last few days. The first week was just ending but it seemed already seemed that everyone had fallen into the school year stupor.

Jerard and I mostly tuned out Shannon as she went through a literal check list in front of her. Paying attention only when we heard our names mentioned. I looked around the cafeteria, in my effort to not listen to her over dramatics about the DJ arriving a half an hour late and having to settle for cucumbers sticks instead of celery in the veggie tray. That's when I saw something that had to be out of the ordinary.

"Aiden." I stared at the double doors leading out to the courtyard, where Sam has just appeared. He didn't say anything and I realized Shannon was still going on and on. "Shan, shut up. Aiden, what's Sam doing here?"

Shannon looked like she'd just been hit with something large and blunt. Apparently you didn't tell her to shut up.

"I have no clue." Aiden, Jerard and I got up and walked over to Sam who was looking in every direction.

"Sammy." I called to him as we approached.

"Thank God, I didn't think I'd ever find you in here. I was hoping you'd be in the courtyard with the temperature being above average today. You see the lack of cloud cover . . ."

"Sam what are you doing here?" I cut him off before he could get going.

"Oh! Sorry! I did some research for you this morning before school." he told me. "About what you've been going through."

"What's he talking about?" Jerard looked between Aiden and I.

"I told them what's been going on. All of it." I explained quickly. "What did you find out?"

"Well, every year there are thousands and thousands of paranormal activities reported. Some are just like what you've experienced, dreams and flashbacks. A lot are sightings of apparitions and EVP . . ." Sam told us.

"EVP?" Aiden quizzed.

"Electronic Voice Phenomenon. This is how it works, you leave say . . . a tape recorder on and you leave the house that's supposedly haunted. When you come back if you have a powerful enough entity you'll be able to hear things going on, on the tape. Voices, foot steps, crying whatever that entity is feeling."

"And this is scientifically proven?" Aiden scoffed.

"Well, no, not scientifically. Paranormal investigators are ever trying to prove the existence of ghosts, spirits and poltergeists. A lot now use scientific methods to tell what are normal every day sounds and what's, well, paranormal."

"So what does this have to do with us?" Jerard asked, curiosity seeming to get the better of him.

"Ghost usually appears when they have unfinished business. Claire's aunt being murdered and never found could be the reason for her contacting you." Sam told us.

"But what about Jer's grandpa?" Aiden asked.

"That one's a tough one to tell. You see, James Davenport lived a long filling life. The only thing I can think of is that the disappearance of his true love had deeply disturbed him and he's here to help."

"So it's really a fluke that we're having all this happen to us?" I asked feeling kind of stupid for believing that maybe Jerard and I had some sort of . . . ability.

"Not entirely. I believe that the reason you two have the flashbacks is because of the blood in you. It's not documented as often but I did find one possibility that because you two share the blood of the deceased, it's easier for them to possess you. They find their strength in your genetic make up and your energy. Though I will admit that is a less likely solution." Sam shook his head.

"Why?" I asked.

"Well, if that were true there'd be people getting haunted all the time by loved ones that have passed on. But it's still a possibility."

"I thought you were a 'scientist' Sam." Aiden eyed his younger brother.

"I am, but part of being a good scientist is being open enough to other possibilities." Sam acknowledged. "I've found a few ways to contact the dead."

"You want to really try to mess with that stuff?" Aiden stared at us incredulously.

"There's a séance, but I don't know that you'd have time for that." Sam ignored Aiden, "There's the Ouija board which could or could not produce proper results, and there's a thing called Automatic writing."

"What's that?" Jerard asked.

"You can't be seriously . . ." Aiden chimed again.

"Shush Aiden," I quieted him. "Let Sam talk."

"It's simple really. It's like an OBE." Sam went on.

"OBE?"

"Out of Body Experience. It's what you had at the lake Claire. You achieved one by off chance, but people really can travel different astral planes. Or at least they believe they do. You have to be in a very relaxed state to even get there usually. It's sort of the same way with automatic writing. You have to be relaxed and let your sub conscious take over. Sit with a pen and a piece of paper and let the words flow. You've seen The Sixth Sense right? That Bruce Willis movie? The little boy did it, he was drawing or something and he starting writing out the argument on the paper. The exact same thing." Sam explained.

"I don't think we'd be able to do that. What else you got?" I sighed.

"Well," Sam looked crestfallen, "there's certain things that happen when the paranormal is about to happen. Um, like the batteries on anything electric draining completely. It takes a lot of energy to have an apparition appear. Or the temperature dropping dramatically. Have you felt like you've been being watched? They say to trust your instincts on that one. They also say that moving objects is a good sign too. And not to state the obvious, but trouble sleeping is a sign too."

"Excuse me, what's this?" Mrs. Lancaster's cold voice surprised us. None of us had an answer for her.

"Mr. Hart, I do believe you are supposed to be at the middle school." Mrs. Lancaster scowled at him.

"I was . . . well you see . . ." Sam stuttered looking at us for help.

"Let's see I believe that's detention for you Mr. Hart, for leaving school. And I think it would do you three well to serve a day or so as well. For luring a younger student out of school." Mrs. Lancaster grinned nastily.

"WHAT?!" we bellowed.

"Would you like two days?" she continued.

"What's going on here?" Mrs. Harper came to the rescue.

"Just enforcing school rules, Angela." Mrs. Lancaster replied.

"Is that so, Dana?" Mrs. Harper raised a brow. "What's going on here, kids?"

"I just wanted to help." Sam looked at Mrs. Harper miserably.

"Help with what, dear?" Mrs. Harper's tone softened.

"Mrs. Lancaster gave them a project on Claire's Aunt Fiona, and Jerard's grandpa was involved and I found some research that I thought they might find helpful. I was so excited I just couldn't wait to tell them. The police report for example. They didn't make me come over here. I came myself – they shouldn't get in trouble because of me."

"You assigned them the Fiona Kelly project?" Mrs. Harper rounded on Mrs. Lancaster. "Sam, get back to the middle school, and check in with Mr. Carpenter, I'll be calling to make sure you return. Jerard, Claire, Aiden, don't worry about detention, go back to your lunch. And Dana, if you'll come with me I believe we need to speak with Jerry." With that Mrs. Lancaster and Mrs. Harper made their way out of the cafeteria. The four of us looked at each other.

"I better get back. I can't believe we all just got out of detention." Sam stared after them.

"Me too." I agreed, Sam hot footed it out the door and we made our way back to the table.

I leaned against the brick wall outside the commons area waiting for Jerard after fifth hour. Most of the school passed through the gym door before Jerard came into view, Aiden and Shannon at his side. Jerard smiled at me, his hand found mine and our fingers intertwined. Aiden and Shannon led the way into the gym, where apparently we were supposed to sit with our class. The freshmen were to our immediate right, and counter clockwise around the gym sat the Sophomores, Juniors and Seniors.

Ryan, Key, Ana and a boy I didn't recognize were sitting at the top of the Northwest corner of the bleachers. Shannon and I sat on either side of Ana, Aiden and Jerard sat behind us with the rest of the boys.

"Hey Claire, this is Declan Sullivan. Dec, this is Claire she's Aiden's step sister." Ana introduced me.

"Hi." I turned to wave at him.

"Hey." he smiled politely.

I was content to lean back against the bench behind me in between Jerard's legs as his long arms draped over my shoulders listening to the pre-pep rally chatter. When Mr. Bishop cleared his throat into a microphone and the chatter died down. He was standing at our end of the gym facing the student body as a whole.

"He gives the same speech every year." Jerard muttered to me, I smirked and ignored Mr. Bishop's supposedly uplifting speech brushing my fingers against Jerard's.

I wasn't really paying attention to the pep rally, that sort of function never being my thing. I was pulled back to reality when Jerard was dragging me to my feet.

"Is it time to go?" I looked at Jerard.

"No, we have to sing." he pointed to a large board on the wall of the gym with the ASH Fight song written on it.

"Ha," I scoffed, "Yeah, that's going to happen."

I covered my ears as my class started to scream the song. Apparently it was a loudness contest, I felt like my ear drums were going to explode as even Jerard was screaming the song. I sank back onto my bench and waited for it to be over.

"What's the matter, Sis? Too loud?" Aiden teased.

"Bad singing." I raised a brow at him pointedly.

This time I vaguely heard the Seniors singing next to us. I wasn't surprised when the Sophomores, who seemed to have the largest class, won. I watched, mildly entertained as groups of six people from each class spelled out ALDEN with their bodies in front of us. As classes raced each other with ridiculous challenges and that sort of thing. Just to pass time I'm sure.

The bell rang and it seemed like the school as a whole got up and started filing out of the gym. Jerard jumped down to walk next to me as we followed the others down the bleachers. He was telling me how he planned to get to the cave when I felt something press against my back sending me forward. I fell in to Declan who was also tall but thick so it didn't effect him, I apologized and turned to look for Jerard, but he wasn't there. Looking around confused, I found Jerard lying on the gym floor, his eyes closed. Our classmates looked around surprised, as I jumped bleachers as many as I could at a time with out killing myself to get to him.

"Jerard? Jerard, can you hear me?" I was kneeling next to him, shaking him gently.

"What's going on here?" Mr. Bishop demanded walking over to us. My friends and other classmates had formed a circle around Jerard and I. *That's a loaded question.*

"Jer tripped coming down the bleachers, sir." Shannon supplied for me.

"Jerard?" I murmured to him, "Please, please, *please* be okay."

"Call an ambulance, Mr. Rexton." Mr. Bishop said assertively, "Miss. Weston, you're free to go. As are all of you." he reminded us.

"I'm not going anywhere" I didn't let go on Jerard's hand.

"This is none of your concern." Mr. Bishop crossed his arms.

"Yes it is!" Shannon snapped, "She's his girlfriend!" I didn't know if that was really my label but I was going with it at that point.

"Beat it, guys." I muttered to Shannon facing them, "Tell Mom and Dad where I am okay?"

"Break it up everyone! Time to go home." Aiden nodded, using his jock popularity, started ushering people away.

Jerard had regained consciousness by the time the paramedics got to the gym. They treated him for a concussion and a few bruises forming on his torso. Then reluctantly released him into my care after speaking to my mom over the phone, promising to look after Jerard this weekend as his Aunt Jodi was out of town.

Jerard was holding an ice pack to his head when he opened the driver's side door to his Jeep, I quickly shut it again.

"Keys." I held my hand out.

"I'm fine, Claire."

"Lets see, ice pack, concussion, bruises." I raised a brow at him. "Keys, I won't crash you're baby I promise."

Sighing Jerard gave me his keys and went around to the other side. I jumped up into the drivers seat, adjusted it, and took off for home stopping by Jerard's house along the way to pick up his stuff for the weekend.

"Did you fall?" I asked as we pulled out of his driveway. He glanced at me for a moment before returning his gaze to the tree lined streets.

"I was pushed."

"Me too." I nodded gravely, "Aunt Fiona said he was after us."

"Almost got me."

Jerard's chest rose and fell steadily as he slept. His concussion had relieved us of any pre-party details that were to be seen to. Shannon expressly told us that Jerard was to go home and relax and I was to keep any eye on him, but we were to be at her house promptly at eight o'clock.

Not being too keen on hanging crepe paper and tying balloons together, I took her up on the offer. Mom fussed over Jerard a bit when we first got to the house, making sure he was okay and trying to get him to eat something. All he wanted to do was lay down, we dropped his stuff in the guest room, but he followed me to my room instead. I didn't mind when he curled up in my bed, I found the nearest book and started reading.

"Claire, honey, why don't you come down for supper?" Mom came into the room. I glanced at Jerard. "I'll grab something at the party."

"You've been up here since you came home." Mom went on. "You should eat something."

"He's alone enough Mom."

"Can I talk to you in the hallway, Claire?" Mom motioned to the door. I had a sinking feeling this was not going to be a good conversation, but followed her into the hallway.

"Is there something going on between you and Jerard? I mean, are you two an 'item'?" Mom inquired.

"I don't know. Maybe? We've been working on a history project is all."

"What history project?" she demanded skeptically. Something in her tone sent me over the edge.

"The one where Aunt Ona went missing." I replied icily.

"Who told you that?" Mom took at step back.

"Everyone. The whole town knows, mom! My friends couldn't believe that *I* didn't know." I crossed my arms hunching my shoulders slightly.

"We didn't so you could have a normal life here." Mom stuttered.

"Whatever."

"Really, we thought it was for the best." I shrugged.

"Claire don't be mad, You didn't even know Fiona." Mom finally snapped.

"That's not the point!" I growled, "The point is, you lied to me and let me come to this town not preparing me for what I might hear." Mom looked at me sadly, but admitted defeat retreating back downstairs. I pivoted and walked back in to my room settling back into my chair.

"She didn't freak out as much as I thought she would." Jerard said. I looked over at him, his eyes weren't even open yet.

"Yeah, I was thinking that too." I sighed. "I was going to wake you in a few, we're due at Shannon's soon."

"What time is it?" Jerard ran hand through his bed head.

"Seven-thirty."

"I'm getting up." Jerard sat up quickly, swinging his feet over the edge of the bed. "Oooo." He held his palm to his head.

"Easy killer." I stood up, "Slow movements."

"Thanks, Doc." he gave me a lopsided grin.

In the living room Sam was looking very disinterested in his Nintendo DS, Jerard looked at me and winked. I stared at him in question as he walked very as-a-matter-of-factly into the living room and plucked the game system out of his hand.

"Lets go." He said.

"Go where?" he jumped in surprise.

"The party."

"I can't go. I'm not in high school." Sam shook his head.

"You're gate crashing. Besides there'll be some kids your age there. A lot of parents will be there and some youngins." Jerard told him. I was leaning in the door way smiling at Jerard.

"Can I Claire?" He looked at me hopefully.

"Well, yeah!" I laughed. "Mom and Dad are probably going to show up later. You may as well come with us."

"Okay! I'll go tell Mom and Dad!" Sam looked really happy for the first time in a while. We waited around for a bit while Sam went to change out of the PJ's he'd already put on.

"You keep an eye on him, Claire!" Mom called to me as we left the house.

"You're going to be thirteen next week," I looked at Sam, "I doubt you'll need too much looking after, right?"

Sam puffed out his chest. "None! I'm big enough to take care of myself."

"I thought so." I nodded approvingly. Obviously I had no intention of letting him run wild but Aiden, in particular, treated Sam like he was five years old still.

The party must have been in full swing by the time we got there, Jerard actually had to park a couple blocks away from Shannon's house! He linked his fingers around mine as we walked along the street. Sam wandering on ahead of us.

"Are you up for this? You look a little pale." I mentioned to him.

"*You* look pale." He grinned at me.

"*I am* pale. But this is a sick kinda pale, like a vampire kinda pale. You're not going to suck my blood are you?" I laughed.

"Don't girls like vampires?"

"I'd prefer to stay living, actually."

"I'm fine though. Don't worry." He squeezed my hand gently. "So have fun tonight. We both could use it."

The Snows had a very large house, but even it seemed to be filled to bursting when we finally walked in. We squeezed through the crowds of people, Sam sticking close to Jerard as we made our way. Jerard, and even Sam seemed to know everyone there. I mostly stood listening to the conversations going on around me. I wasn't eavesdropping it was more like a buzz in the ear to keep myself entertained.

"Claire!" Key's head appeared over everyone else.

"Key!" I hugged him gratefully. "I don't know anyone here." He shrugged, "You will soon enough. Hey Jer, I'm stealing your girlfriend."

"Huh?" Jerard looked up, "Oh okay, have fun."

"Where are you stealing me away to?" Key grabbed my hand and led me through the throngs of people in the house.

"Ryan and Ana and the rest are outside. Jer always talks to the parents." Key called back to me as he got closer to the DJ playing some random Pop song. Though, it was slow moving, he had a pretty good grip on me so I didn't get lost as we made our way through the house and out into the back yard.

Mr. Snow was surrounded by a group of older men showing off his grill mastery, making jokes and serving up fresh from the grill hamburgers, hot dogs and brats. He seemed to be the life of the party for the over eighteen crowd, not that it surprised me. In the house, Haylee was the perfect hostess moving from group to group to keep up appearances.

"Hi Claire!" Shannon's dad waved his grill tongs at me.

"Hi Mr. Snow!" I called back to him as someone jumped in the pool.

"There you are! How's Jer? Where have you guys been?" It sounded like one big word as fast as Shannon was saying it.

"Hey, wait." I pointed to the pool. "I thought people didn't swim at pool parties?" Shannon rolled her eyes, "You don't if you don't want to wash off your make up!"

"Oh. How stupid of me." I raised a brow at her, "Jerard's okay. Some scratches and bruises. He's in the house, Key saved me from boredom. We brought Sammy."

"Oh, cool, Aiden's around here somewhere. I think he's off getting drinks." Shannon looked around, but Aiden was nowhere in sight. "Ana! Claire's here!" Ana came bouncing towards me, Declan on her heels.

"You made it! How's Jer? We didn't think you were going to make it. Jer looked horrible." Ana hugged me.

"He's okay. No sudden movements though. Hey Declan." I added a greeting to him as he hovered near the rim of our group.

"Hey Claire." he nodded. "Good to see you in one piece."

"Thanks to you." I grinned at him. He waved me off laughing.

"Its good to know I'm good for something."

"Aha." Ana shifted uncomfortably. "Dec, why don't we go find something to drink, anyone want anything?" Ana touched his forearm. I stared up at Key confused as she and Declan walked off.

"Guys think you're hot, Claire, and the news of you and Jerard hasn't really spread yet." Key shrugged.

"Jerard and I aren't *officially* anything." I told him.

"Okay, go hug up on Ryan and see what Jer does." Key nodded at Ryan, who was chatting up a pretty redheaded girl near the pool.

"Yeah, that probably wouldn't be a good idea." Aiden appeared over Shannon's shoulder. "Jer's not a jealous guy but that might be asking for it."

"Hey Aiden." I greeted, "Yeah, I didn't really want to test that theory."

"Women." Key shook his head playfully. I reached over and punched him in the shoulder.

"Yeah, yeah."

Aiden was surprisingly cool that night. I never thought I'd say it but my "near death experience" was probably one of the best things that had happened to me. Aiden seemed to warm up to me, Jerard had chosen to be with me, and Shannon and Ana seemed to have become amazing friends that I was sure I could talk to about just about everything.

The party was nearing the midway point when all the drama started. What? Did you honestly think I was going to have a night of teenage normalcy? If nothing else I've learned that life in Alden's Hollow was going to be anything but normal. While Persephone was at the party, she kept her distance, content to glare at me from across the pool, it was my own Mom who started it this time. Key and I were making our way back into the house when we heard shouting. In the living room, my mom was being held back by another parent, shouting at someone we couldn't see yet.

"How dare you!" she bellowed as we made our way to closer. "How *dare* you tell her?"

"She needed to know about all the lies you were telling her!" Another woman screamed back. Key and I pushed through to the front of the sea of people. The woman Mom was screaming at was Mrs. Lancaster.

"She is not your daughter!" Mom screamed, "Your father made his mistakes! Don't punish my daughter for them!"

"My father was an innocent man!"

"You are blinded by your hate!" Tears were now streaming down Mom's face. "All these years you still hate my family. *We* never pressed charges, Dad respected him!"

Sam sidled up next to me. "What's going on?"

'Mom's freaking out."

"Why?" Sam gave me a terrified look as Mom and Mrs. Lancaster continued to bellow at each other.

"Key" I nodded at Sam and hurried out to Mom. "Mom!" Mom looked at me but I wasn't so sure she was seeing me.

"Mom, where's dad?" I asked as Mrs. Lancaster continued to scream things.

"Claire?" she looked at me hazily. I put my hands on her shoulders to steady her.

"LANDON!" I screamed, "Aiden! Sam!" Aiden and Sam broke through the people surrounded us.

"Where's dad?" I asked Aiden.

"Out back with Mr. Snow." Sam supplied for him. Aiden tried to say something but he was drown out by Mom yelling over us to Mrs. Lancaster.

"I'm going to get her out of here." I put a hand to my ear. "Tell Shannon, I'm sorry."

"Jer went to get his car. I'll tell dad." Aiden nodded.

"Mom, Mom? Come on. Let's go." I made her look at me. "We're leaving." She looked miserable, but nodded. "Sam, take her out, I'll be out front in a bit." Sam nodded and led mom out of the room. I waited for Sam to leave the room before marching over to Mrs. Lancaster.

"You are a hate filled woman. Your father is dead and I'm sorry about that but don't make everyone else miserable because you can't accept the past. Go to therapy, *after* you apologize to Haylee for ruining her party." She called something after me but only the other party guests heard.

Outside Mom was staring stonily out into the street, Sam standing nervously by. At that moment Jerard pulled up in front of the house. I had to admit, that boy had perfect timing.

"Sam, go find Aiden and Dad, me and Jerard will get her home." I patted him on the shoulder. He looked between Mom and I before nodding and walking back up to the house.

"Come on Mom, we're going home." I took her by the arm. She looked at me uncertainly.

"Okay."

Jerard was out of the car already and opening the back passenger door for her when we got out into the street.

"Thanks, Jerard." I looked at him weakly. The trip home was cold and uneasy, Mom looked as if she were about to break down at any moment and Jerard kept glancing in the rear view mirror at her.

"I'm sorry Claire, I really am." She apologized as I helped her into the house.

"Don't worry about it, Mom." I shook my head.

"But they're all your classmates, I never meant to embarrass you." Mom looked really defeated. Jerard followed behind trying not to impose on mother/daughter time.

"I don't care what those people think of me." I told her. "Besides I think they're a little more surprised by Mrs. Lancaster than you. They all know her."

"I'm so sorry." was all she could mutter as I led her into her bedroom. I stayed with her until Landon got home a few minutes later.

"I'll take care of her, Claire, why don't you go join your brothers and Jer. They're picking out a movie to watch."

"Okay." I lingered on Mom for a moment but left the room.

In the living room Sam, Jerard and Aiden were crowded around the DVD rack. I fell onto the couch pulling out my cell phone. Two text messages had been sent to it while I'd been sorting out Mom. Both from Shannon.

MSG 1: Shannon – What happened?!
MSG 2: Shannon – Where are you?

I wasn't ready to deal with everyone from the party yet. I just turned off my phone.

"Holy cow!" Sam jumped back in surprise, "Where did you come from?"

I looked up at him, "Sorry, I just kinda sneak in." behind him Jerard and Aiden looked at me.

"Shannon's coming over after the party lets out." He turned back to the rack. "She's staying over."

"Quality make out time scheduled?" I smiled at him. Aiden laughed but didn't answer. Sam looked a little grossed out.

"Busted." Jerard knocked him in the shoulder. "So what are you guys feeling? Horror? Comedy? Romance?"

"Anything." I shrugged, I had a feeling I wouldn't be paying attention to it anyway. The boys finally decided on some horrible slasher flick, and I decided to supply the popcorn. I put the bag in the microwave just as Landon came into the kitchen.

"How's Mom?"

"Sleeping now." Landon looked like he was feeling awkward. "She didn't mean to cause a scene, you know that right?"

"I know, I'm not mad. I did think it'd be Persephone causing all the action though." I gave a weak laugh.

"Bill Adams' girl?" he raised a brow.

"Maybe?"

"What's her problem? Is she bullying you?" his tone became a bit harsh.

"She's just mad because Jerard likes me and not her." I shrugged and the microwave beeped. I poured the popcorn into a large green bowl and left before Landon had any time to question. I set the bowl on the coffee table, easily accessible to Sam who was laying on the floor. Aiden was laying on the couch, Jerard sat on the love seat half slouched down.

"There's a spot for you here." Jerard patted the spot on the couch next to him. I laughed softly, but fell into the spot next to him anyway.

"Is she okay?" Jerard pulled me into his arms.

"Yeah, she went to bed." I curled up into his chest.

"Are *you* okay?"

"Today's kinda been a blur. I'll get back to you in the morning." I shut my eyes and fell into a content sleep only to be woken again an hour and a half later when Shannon came in the house.

"Everyone's talking about the fight!" Shannon burst into the living room.

"Shan," Aiden stood up and touched a finger to her lips, "Shh, Mom's sleeping." Shannon gulped, "Sorry."

"What has everyone been saying?" I looked up from my spot on Jerard's chest.

"That Mrs. Lancaster is crazy, she wasn't even supposed to be at the party." Shannon replied, "I can't believe she crashed it and made a scene."

"That makes sense to me, that she's crazy I mean." I scowled. Shannon and I watched as Sam took on Aiden and Jerard in Mario Kart for Wii. Us girls sat on the couch and Shannon filled me in on everything that had happened at the party after we left. Apparently Mr. Snow had to toss Mrs. Lancaster out of the party and round everyone up again.

"Sorry we ruined your party, Shan." I looked at her tiredly.

"Are you kidding? It's going to be the talk of town!" Shannon laughed, "Don't even stress!"

"I'm going to bed kids." Landon came in.

"Goodnight Dad." we chimed, even Jerard and Shannon. He laughed shaking his head and leaving the room.

Aiden and Shannon only waited a half an hour before disappearing upstairs and into his bedroom. Sam left too claiming he wanted to get a head start on a bit of homework, leaving Jerard and I alone in the living room.

"We never did go to that cave." Jerard, who was laying with his head in my lap, pointed out twisting his neck slightly to look at me properly.

"I know. I swear it's got to be connected somehow. I think you're grandpa is messing with my dreams now." I absently stroked his hair, "It didn't feel like it was Ona." Jerard was contemplative for a few moments, though about what was anyone's guess. Finally he swung his feet over the side of the couch and sat up quickly, holding his head as he did.

"Not a good idea." He leaned his elbows on his knees placing his head in his hands for a moment before getting up slowly.

"Where are you going?" I tilted my head at him.

"The more appropriate question is where are *we* going." Jerard put his shoes on. "Get your shoes." By this point I'd learned it was easier not to question.

"Flashlights?" he asked a few moments later as I was tying my own shoes.

"Um," I stopped in the process straightening up. "I think there's a couple in the kitchen, second drawer next to the refrigerator."

"Okay." Jerard went off in search of the flashlights while I went upstairs to grab a hoodie each for Jerard and I. We met in the hallway near Aiden's room. He grinned at me as I cringed and knocked on his door.

"Go. Away." he growled.

"Aiden, unglue yourself and open the damn door." I replied impatiently, Jerard and I stifled laughter as we heard a moment of scrambling and the door opened just enough for Aiden to poke his head through.

"What?" he snapped.

"Jer and I are going out. Cover for us." with that I pressed Jerard's hoodie into his hands and walking down the stairs.

"Do you really think that he's gonna cover for us?" he asked following me down the stairs. I stopped at the bottom and looked at him.

"Good point." I nodded as I heard something fall in the kitchen. "Plan B." I walked in to find that Sam was digging into the last of the pizza that Mom and Landon had ordered for supper. "Hey Sammy." Sam dropped his piece of pizza in surprise.

"Where are you going?" he eyed our flashlights.

"Just out for a bit, we won't be long. Just make something up if mom and dad wake up okay?" Looking suspicious he agreed. "Okay, I'll figure something out."

"Thanks Sammy, you rock." I ruffled his hair before leaving the house.

The streets looked like something out of that stupid horror movie we'd watched earlier. Not that I saw all that much, but it was lit only dimly by street lamps and nothing seemed to be moving. All we needed as for a psycho to come barreling out of the neighbors garage or something and the scene would be complete. Jerard started the Jeep and drove away from the house as slowly as he could trying not to wake Mom and Landon. I had a weird feeling about tonight. I couldn't put my finger on it, but I was sure something was going to happen. Whether it was going to be good or bad was to be determined later.

I grabbed the flashlights as Jerard pulled his hoodie on out by the cliffs. Having no clue where we were about to set off to, I waited at the hatch for him. When he came around to meet me, I handed him a flashlight and we set off to the through the woods. The path wasn't very clear so there were still roots and branches sticking up all over the place. Being accident prone I started to wonder if my weird feeling was about me going to break something.

"What was that look earlier?" Jerard turned to me casually.

"What look?"

"When we were all playing Mario Kart."

"Oh, nothing." I lied through my teeth.

"Almost a longing look," he went on, "You don't even like video games." Jerard continued on trying to coax it out of me in his ever subtle fashion until finally I gave in.

"Okay, Okay, if I tell you will you shut up?"

"Sure." I sighed, "I dunno Jer, sometimes I feel like an outsider at home. I'm a Weston in a house of Hart's. Aiden's finally warmed up to me, I want us to be a family. A proper family." He waited for me to go on.

"Maybe I'm just being stupid." I shrugged.

"No, that's understandable." Jerard said after a moment. "Why don't you ask Landon to adopt you?" He turned to face me.

"No way." I tripped over a root, Jerard, always quick on his feet caught me.

"Steady?" he was very close to me. I hated how he sometimes made me forget what I was thinking.

"I . . . um, yeah." I shook my head,

"So what's the problem with my solution?" he held onto me for a moment longer before leading the way again. "You're dad died years ago, I don't see it."

"I don't know, I guess the way I see it, if Landon wanted to . . . he would have suggested it. Don't you think?"

"I," he spun around and walked backwards casually, "think you should talk to Landon about it. I know he loves you like you're his own daughter."

"You're going to fall." I mentioned shining the light on the path in front of him.

"No I'm not." he shook his head, which made it even funnier when he tripped over a larger rock sticking out of the ground behind him.

"So I'm going to savor the I-told-you-so-moment." I giggled kneeling down next to him. "Are you okay? Did you hit your head?"

"My ego's worse off than I am." Jerard admitted. I grinned at him taking his face in my hands and kissed his forehead.

"Don't worry, I won't tell anyone." I helped him up. The cave wasn't hard to find after Jerard quit goofing around.

"Don't disturb the bats." he warned shining the flashlight up at the ceiling of the cave sure enough it was littered with gross looking bats. Cringing a little I hurried him along the passage way until we hit the large open cavern.

"If my dream was right, the tunnel they took should be right over there." the beam from my flashlight slid across the rock walls and fell on two other large rocks blocking where the tunnel should have been.

"Its sealed." my shoulders slumped a little.

"You're sure?" he looked at me, I nodded, and Jerard set his flashlight on the ground so he could push at the rocks.

"I don't think that's going to work . . ." I mentioned slowly, Jerard ignored me and kept at the rock. After a few moments I noticed my flashlight start to flicker and eventually go out completely.

"Claire," he groaned, "What the hell?"

"I didn't turn it out!" I anxiously shook the light trying to make it come back on, finally it did. Both of our jaws dropped when we noticed that one of the big rocks covering the entrance had slid to the left leaving just enough space for us to pass through.

"How did that happen?" Jerard swallowed hard.

"I-I don't know."

"I guess we can go in now . . ." Jerard tilted his head at the opening, all I could do was nod before following him. We moved along the passage way created by tall rock walls and either side of us I couldn't even tell how deep in we were when Jerard sucked in a long gasp.

"I remember." he mumbled, as I followed him deeper into the cavern.

"Remember what, Jer?"

"We were at the cliffs that day, Charlie, Ona and me. Ona loved going there." His voice was hollow, "She said it was like being in Ireland again. Her parents had taken her there when she was young. She said the way the water hit the rocks was so soothing to her."

"Jerard, you didn't know Fiona." I reminded him apprehensively. Slowly Jerard turned to look at me, in the glow of the flashlight his eyes looked slightly glazed.

"I am not my grandson. Corporal James Davenport" Jerard – James – extended a hand to me, I stood stock still unable to move, "Yes, you would be alarmed." He seemed to come to the realization that it wasn't normal for ghosts or spirits, or whatever he may be didn't materialize in the form of my boyfriend, coming a halt near the end of the cavern. "No need to fear, my dear."

"Fiona, your aunt," he smiled, "You remind me of her so, it's almost as if . . . Anyway, we brought you together, hoping you'd find her. She's lost, like me, I've been following you as much as I can, you and Jerard. When you came here, I felt her, I knew she was here. We can't go on with out each other." I watched Jerard turn to look at whatever it was that he was hiding. "I didn't know that it was me. That I was the one who killed her, but please don't judge me too harshly young Claire."

"Judge you?" I stammered.

"Things that happened in Korea, things I couldn't talk about in life to anyone but your aunt. She was such a loving person, even after she knew what I had done to that man in the river, she still loved me unconditionally. I'm just as bad as Curtis Mitchell said I was. A card shark, I'd buy alcohol in Tokyo and sell it at twice the price, and so much more. You have to understand, it was for her, for Fiona. She was such a good woman, she deserved so much more, a better quality of life than I could give her." James hung his head, "Even on my best day I wasn't nearly good enough for her, but she chose me. I was . . . intoxicated by her."

"I received half of my scars," He pulled up his hoodie to show where the bruises Jerard had received earlier had turned into thin lines where cuts would have been. "are from guys in my unit. Richard Taylor, they man they said killed her, had long arms. He was still in the States but my colonel was friends with him. That's why he hated me so. He was one of those guys who bled not only red, but white and blue too. I wanted to serve my country, I wanted to keep it safe for Fiona."

"That night, we were cliff diving. Ona was a weak swimmer but Charlie and I figured if we were there to help her, it'd be safe. She was on her fourth jump when it happened. I blacked out. When I came to we were heading for Charlie's house. He explained to me that Ona had gone home and we needed to get to his house to fix something on his car. I think I – I killed her Claire, I didn't mean to though I swear!"

I tried to see around James. "I know."

"No," James pressed against my shoulders, "You shouldn't see her like this. You look so much like her, like Jerard does me. You must listen, Claire. I don't blame Charlie, he was trying to protect me. The loyalties we had to each other didn't stay in Korea. What you would call it now, Post Traumatic Stress Syndrome, it was barely thought of then, let alone a possible defense. Promise me something, Claire?"

"What?"

"Give her a proper burial, she deserves that." I nodded mutely.

"Jerard will watch over you much better than I watched over your aunt. I can see it inside of him. It's not just us that brought you together."

I was still trying to sort out what he meant exactly when Jerard heaved and fell to the ground. He was rubbing his head, looking confused in the near darkness. I knelt down next to him.

"What happened?"

"I don't think I should explain here." Thrown into sharp reality, Jerard followed my horrified gaze to a pile of fabric and bone.

"Is that what . . . who I think it is?"

Jerard and I stumbled back into the house twenty minutes later, not bothering to keep the noise down. The silence in the car was deafening, I was glad to hear the TV going in the living room.

"Claire? Jerard?" Sam came into the entry way. "It's about time. Mom woke up, she was gonna go into your room but I told her than you were in the bathroom."

"Good job, Sammy." I replied, "You're amazing."

"You guys look awful, where were you?" Sam watched us taking off our shoes.

"Just out at the cliffs." Jerard put his hand on my shoulder. Sam looked as if he didn't believe us but went back into the living room. "Come on, love."

Jerard led me up to the stairs and into my room. He told me put my pajamas on and he'd be in to tuck me in in a few minutes. Feeling emotionally and physically exhausted I had a bit of trouble pulling them on. It took me a few moments to realize that my shirt was on backwards. It was just hitting me how warm my pajamas were against my chilled skin from the cave, when I realized Shannon wasn't in my room yet. Praying that Aiden wasn't molesting her I turned off the light and slipped into bed. My thick comforter was wonderfully warm and I was beginning to think that I would fall asleep before Jerard came into say goodnight.

I was almost out when I heard my door open. My eyes fluttered open and Jerard's outline was silhouetted only briefly before he shut the door behind him. He didn't say anything but curled up next to me and let me rest my head on his chest.

"It'll be okay, Claire." His hands slid through my hair. "We'll figure it out tomorrow."

"I'm just glad it's over." I murmured.

SATURDAY

AUNT ONA WAS dead. Her body was hanging limp in James' arms. Charlie was moving ahead of them whistling merrily. What the hell was wrong with this guy?

"Just a bit further Jim." He told James. "Almost there."

"We never bury the wounded." James told him.

"Special case. Here, set 'er – I mean him here." Robotically, James set her down not questioning his friend.

"Good. Now come on." Charlie ushered James out of the cave and back onto the beach. James' eyes seemed to slide back into focus.

"Where's Ona?" he looked up at Charlie, who was a few inches taller.

"She went home." Charlie told him, "We should get going. We gotta go look at that fan belt."

"Oh. Okay, yeah. Lets go." James looked confused but followed his Army buddy.

After a while I felt my source of heat disappear and I woke again. Dazed a little, I stared around the darkened room, Shannon was sleeping on an air mattress, glancing at my clock it read five o'clock. Grumbling softly I shrugged the covers off of me and slid out of bed. My head was spinning with the memories of just hours ago fresh in my mind.

I moved silently down the hallway towards Jerard's room, pressed open the door, slipped inside and glanced at mom and Landon's door as I closed it behind me. Jerard was shirtless, sleeping on his stomach, and his longer hair had fallen across his face. I smiled to myself in the moonlight before crawling into the full size bed beside him. He lifted his head sleepily when he felt my weight beside him.

"Claire?" his voice was groggy, "Are you okay, love?"

"I didn't want to be alone."

In the darkness Jerard kissed my forehead and cradled me satisfyingly close. I really didn't want to talk about it, but Jerard had no recollection of what he – James – had said in the cave. As I often had to, I built myself up and let the whole story barrel out before I could change my mind, pausing only to take a deep breath before diving deep into another part of the story. Jerard listened intently never interrupting, but it was clear he was trying to sift through it all. We laid in silence for quite sometime, until we heard movement in the hallway. Assuming it was Landon, I waited for the footsteps to go down the stairs and I sneaked back to my room, only to fall back into an uneasy sleep.

"Claire! Time to get up!" Shannon bounced onto my bed.

"Shan, I swear, if it's before eleven o'clock . . ." I threatened turning over to look at my clock. It was suddenly noon, I gathered my hair over one shoulder and turned back to Shannon.

"You're not pregnant, are you?" I vaguely remembered the annoyed look on Aiden's face the night before.

"No! Of course not!" Shannon looked scandalized, "Are you?"

"V-card still in tact." I replied.

"Good. Come on, get out of bed, we're supposed to meet everyone at six we need to start getting ready."

"Hey, you go on ahead, I need to take care of some stuff before we go to the festivities. I'll be back in time for you to make me your dress up doll, don't worry."

Jerard held my hand as we walked up the stone steps into the police station. Not many people were milling around but we did find a younger officer sitting at his desk.

"Weekender, Officer?" Jerard asked conversationally.

"Yes sir." The name plate on his desk named him Officer Eric Martin. "What can I do for you kids?"

"I'm Jerard Lane and this is Claire Weston, sir." Jerard nodded. Officer Martin shuffled some paperwork. Jerard glanced at me.

"We think we may have found Fiona Kelly."

"You two have found her, when my Uncle, one of the finest officers in the department couldn't?" Officer Martin scoffed.

"Yes, sir, I don't think she would have been easy to find by anyone."

Officer Martin looked annoyed but curious at the same time. He listened to our story and even went out to the cave after some begging from us. He looked like he'd won the lottery when he found my Aunt's bones, and Jerard and I didn't bother to hide our disgust with him as he was practically skipping back to the cave entrance. I could only minimally relate to him in the aspect that he'd solved a case that was in the family. Half of the cops on duty in Alden's Hollow came out to the cave, but the time afternoon hit any one over forty five years old seemed to have gathered behind the yellow tape line wondering if the mystery of Fiona Kelly had really been solved. Seeing as we were witnesses and not suspects we managed to keep Mom and Landon out of the picture, I didn't want to think what kind of shape Mom would be in if they called her. We left as soon as they would let us, neither of us liking the sudden shove into the lime light. We were at home for less than an hour, playing a game of LIFE with Aiden, Shannon and Sam when Landon found out.

"Turn on channel three." Landon came into the living room, his phone to his ear. Aiden reached for the remote and flipped the TV on switching it to the right channel.

"The remains are believed to be those of Fiona Mary Kelly. A youth that went missing in 1951, though that report has not been confirmed. A crime lab in Oakdale is working right now to identify the body. Join us at six for more."

"I saw it Jeff, thanks. I'll talk to you later." Landon hung up the phone and glanced at me before calling to my mother. "Amelia?" Mom walked into the room and looked at him expectantly.

"They think they found Fiona." He mentioned almost nervously. Mom's eyes flicked almost nervously between Landon and I.

"Before you freak out." I sat forward, "You should know that it was Jerard and I found the body – er bones."

Mom's face was a mix of terror and sorrow. We explained to her the story we told the police, we were out hiking that morning when Jerard took me into the cave. Mom apologized several times for us having to go through that, but she was proud of me for taking everything in such a grown up manner and kept rambling until Aiden thankfully stepped in.

"Um, Mom, We have to meet everyone soon."

"Yeah, and I have to make her pretty." Shannon put her hands on my shoulders.

"Thanks, Shan." I looked up at her sarcastically, though it got mom off my back and Shannon and I were allowed to move upstairs to my room. Once the door was securely shut I let out a sigh of relief.

"You're a life saver."

"No problem. Time to get pretty!" Shannon waved off my thank you but became giddy at the idea of clothes and make up. That was the cool thing about Shannon though. When it came right down to it, she knew when to let something go. Shannon started digging through my closet trying to find something acceptable.

"You have a *Louis Vutton*?" Her eyes were wide when she hit the boxes at the bottom of my closet. I looked up from the magazine I was reading on my bed.

"Oh, yeah, my Aunt Eleanor works in New York for some big advertising firm. She thinks I'm a girlie girl." I shrugged, "Louis Vutton, Prada, Chanel, Dolce and Gabbana."

"I – you're – Claire!" she sputtered, "I would kill for a purse like this."

"Take it, or any of the others, except the Prada one, I actually like that one." I went back to my magazine, but only after I saw her face light up. I looked up from time to time as she modeled the different bags in my full length mirror.

"Should I pick out my own outfit?" I asked as she tried on the Chanel bag for the third time.

"No! I think I like this one, are you sure Claire? These are really expensive purses . . ." Shannon faced me with an apprehensive look on her face.

"Go ahead ever since Nicole Kidman became a Chanel spokeswoman I haven't really liked the line." I assured her, "I told you, you just can't have the Prada one."

"Thanks, Claire!" Shannon nearly knocked me off the bed with the force that she hugged me with.

"No problem." I choked, "Uh, Shan, air is a necessity."

"Sorry." She let me go. "You just rock."

"I know. If you don't get moving I'm going like this." I threatened looking at the clock.

"Okay, okay!" Shannon jumped off the bed and back into my closet. Rolling my eyes, and watched her tear through my clothes, pick out a pair of blue jeans, and a tan sweater and start digging into her own duffle bag.

"What are you looking for?" I tilted my head at her. Shannon didn't respond as I changed my outfit.

"Here, wear that with this." Shannon tossed me a bright pink vest with a fur lined hood. I stared at it for a moment before tossing it back to her.

"No way, I draw the line at fake fur. This is fine."

"Okay, I'll wear it then." Shannon shrugged, I sat down at my vanity, rolling my eyes, while Shannon changed behind me.

The longer I tried to do my hair the more nothing looked right. So I decided to just flip the ends out and call it good. Shannon invaded with her make up bag and though she looked like Miss. Teen USA already, Shannon proceeded to change spots with me and reapply every bit of make up she already had on. I looked her over as I waited, she had demanded that I wait for her to 'descend.' She was in blue jeans and white long sleeved shirt that contrasted greatly with her bright pink vest, to top it all off she actually wore fur covered boots that looked like they'd be more fitting for a yeti as opposed to a night out with friends.

"Alright boys!" Shannon jumped the last two stairs into her best 'ta da!' pose, "We're ready!"

Behind Aiden, I heard Jerard try to cover a laugh by coughing, I followed his gaze to Shannon's boots and grinned at him.

We walked along the path between The Servant's Barrel and the small alterations shop next door. Shannon, in all her model-esque glory, walked arm in arm with Aiden, Jerard allowed me to lead the way holding my hand lightly. The closer we came, the louder the voices on Main Street became. I never knew so many people actually lived in Alden's Hollow. The street was packed with food, vendors, carnival games, and even on the porch of the Servant's Barrel a small band was set up playing music for a packed dance floor in the middle of the street.

"Hi ladies!" Ana rushed forward and hugged me and Shannon excitedly in turn.

"Hey Ana," I managed to catch the piece of cherry pie that Jerard and I were sharing as it teetered dangerously. "Hey Dec." Declan grinned at me looking really rather embarrassed.

"Pie!" Ryan pounced on a piece of pumpkin, Key on a piece of blueberry before they greeted me with an awkward hug and Jerard a handshake.

"The whole town is going crazy." Key said through a mouthful of pie as we moved along the street. "They found Fiona Kelly."

"We know, Claire and Jerard found her." Aiden retorted, Jerard and I shifted uncomfortably as all eyes focused on us. So once again we dived into the tale, giving the edited version. No one had to know that we were communicating with the dead, not that any of them would believe us anyway.

"Wow, Mrs. Lancaster is kinda screwed up, I mean even more now." Declan let out a low whistle after everything had sunk in.

"How did you stay so . . . normal? I would have been freaking out!" Ana clutched on to Declan's arm, I grinned at her, she was using it as an excuse to touch him and it worked. Declan reached up and took her hand.

"I've been telling him that she's nuts all along." I followed as they moved off along the road again, our group kept getting separated by all the people in the street. So I fell back to talk with Shannon and Ana who were giggling to each other after I ditched my empty pie plate.

"What are you two giggling about?" I slid in between the two.

"Ana and Declan." Shannon supplied shortly.

"Ah, how's the date going?" I smirked at Ana, "Declan's kinda hot."

"I know!" Ana gushed, "When he picked me up? Oh-my-god."

"But you've got Jer, so how could anyone compare?" Shannon nudged me.

"Shut up, Shan. Get me up to speed, what's going on?" I smacked her in the arm.

"He picked me up and brought me daisies, and my dad? Get this, he actually likes him! We just got here when we ran into Key and Ryan. Who were naturally dateless. Then we found you guys."

"So what are you doing back here and giggling with us, and not up there hugging up on him?" I nodded in Declan's direction. She grinned at me, and I nudged her forward. Falling into step between Jerard and Ryan, I looped my arms in each of theirs and realized they were talking about the football game.

As we wandered through the streets with my new friends, I felt truly at home for the first time. It was amazing how much easier it was to fit in when you weren't feeling like an outsider because of a relative you've never met. We stopped to play a few games, and sample a few of the other vendors adventures in cooking. I watched as Ana and Shannon had little hearts painted on their cheeks at the face painting booth, each of the guys took turns having their photos taken in those little cardboard stand ups that you put only your face into, of a strong man from the twenties, we were making out way back down the street towards the Servant's Barrel when Shannon spotted the old time photo trailer parked in front of Allie's bookshop.

"Come on guys!" Shannon pulled me and Aiden by the hands into the long trailer. There wasn't much room for all of us in there with the long 1920's speak easy scene at the other end of the trailer and the large camera.

"Can you fit eight of us?" Ana asked 'Hi my name is Chloe'.

"Yes we can!" she boomed jovially. Lets get the ladies settled first. Gentlemen, if you don't mind." She waved them out of the door way and shut it behind us. Ana, Shannon and I had fun watching each other slip into the different colored flapper style dresses. I laughed as I noticed that even though the photos would in black and white, Shannon insisted on having a bright pink dress.

"Alright girls," Hi my name is Chloe finished tying the back of my dress. "Go stand near the bar, and we'll get the boys in here." Chloe went to call the boys back in as Ana, Shannon and I maneuvered around the camera and went to stand around the bar. We were admiring each other's costumes when the cat calls started.

"Ow ow!" Ryan cooed. The other boys, Jerard included, followed suit. Ana and I turned bright red, but Shannon reveled in the attention modeling for the boys.

"Does she not get enough attention at home?" I grinned at Ana. Ana rolled her eyes as she shook her head. The boys dressed in pinstripe suits and fedoras and joined us one at a time as Hi my name is Chloe okayed their outfits.

"You have great legs." Jerard muttered to me. On reflex I swatted him on the arm.

"Shut up."

"Just saying . . ."

"Alright girls up on the bar." Hi my name is Chloe instructed, Jerard, Declan and Aiden helped us up onto the bar and waited for Hi my name is Chloe to position the boys around us. She handed us fake guns and money bags, told us to smile and snapped a few photos for safety before we were allowed to get changed again. Jerard, Key and I loitered outside while the others waited for the photos to be printed.

"If that really is Fiona Kelly, this place is gonna be crazy." Key mentioned as the wind blew his loose long hair around his face.

"It is." I said somberly, Jerard reached for my hand. Key nodded looking like he was feeling awkward.

"Sorry, Claire." He mumbled, I patted him on the shoulder. "I hope so."

"Here they are!" Shannon bounded out of the trailer and handed us each our copy of the photograph.

"Thanks, Shan." We chorused. It was nearing nine o'clock when we found our way back to the Servant's Barrel. The band was in full swing and people of all ages were dancing in the open area in front of the porch.

"This is awesome." I enjoyed seeing everyone dancing and having a good time. We didn't have anything like this back in Oakdale.

"May I?" Key offered his hand to me.

"You dance?"

"Call me Fred Astaire." Key took my hand and twirled me under his arm before leading me onto the dance floor. I vaguely heard Ryan ask our friends who Fred Astaire was. The song was slow and very pretty, and Key was right, he was quite light on his feet.

"Its weird, Fiona and James, you and Jerard." Key commented as we avoided bumping into other dancers. "I hope history isn't repeating itself."

"Doubtful, but I'm sure they had a hand in it." I replied elusively. Key tilted his head at me, but I was content to steer the conversation in another direction. "I'm so glad this week is over."

"I bet. By Monday everything will be back to normal." Key nodded, I hoped he was right.

"If Mrs. Lancaster hasn't been fired or anything. Is that too much to hope?" I adjusted my hand in his.

"Maybe." he smiled. "They might let you switch you out of her class though."

"I couldn't get that lucky."

He laughed. "So things are going okay with you and Jer?"

"I guess?" I laughed, "What's your thing with making sure that me and Jerard end up together?" He shrugged.

The song ended and Key and I were headed back to our group when I was grabbed by the wrist and brought back onto the dance floor. I'm not sure how long I'd been swept around the dance floor before I could focus on who I'd been stolen by.

"Hi Charlie." I was surprised but the ease in which he moved to the lively tune.

"I am sorry for the abrupt snatching, but you're helping me make all the other old codgers jealous right now."

"I'm glad to be of service." I laughed feeling a little unnerved. Charlie nodded and grinned widely.

"Did you hear that they may have found my Aunt's body?" I went on conversationally.

"Oh, did they?" he cleared his throat.

"Yep."

"Where did they find her?"

"In a half blocked cavern in a cave near the Cliffs. Where you and James left her." I tried to sound conversational as opposed to accusing. He stopped dead (no pun intended) though his face didn't contort in anyway.

"Trying to steal my girl, Charlie?" Jerard wrapped his arm around my waist.

"Not at all, she's all yours." Charlie gave me a dark look and walked away.

"What was that all about?" he looked at me, I shrugged indifference was better than the truth right now. I saw Ana make her way through the crowd of dancers towards us.

"Come on, we're all heading over to Ryan's to watch movies." Ana told us excitedly.

"So that means cuddle time for you and Dec?" I grinned at her.

"Claire!" her eyes shifted from me to Jerard.

"Jerard doesn't care!" I laughed as we followed her back through the crowd.

Mr. and Mrs. Winters were decidedly plain next to their heartthrob son, and their about-to-be-crowned-miss-America daughter, Kate. They were also two of the nicest people you could ever hope to meet. I mean how many parents opened their home to several teenagers on a whim, and supplied them with pop and pizza to boot? Our group had swelled a little, I noticed, as we all gathered in the living room to watch a set of horror movies. Key and Ryan had produced some guy Ryan introduced only as Dylan out of nowhere it seemed. Twenty minutes into the most confusing low budget horror film known to man kind, Jerard and I decided to join Mr. and Mrs. Winters, who were playing cribbage in the kitchen.

"So they found Fiona Kelly after all these years." Mr. Winters said conversationally. "Though I bet you don't know much about that, do you Claire?"

"Actually, she was my aunt sir, I'm Amelia Kelly's daughter."

"Oh." He looked slightly guilty.

"It's okay, I'm not overly effected by it. I never met her . . . obviously." I laughed nervously.

"Oh, well that was quite the scandal. Finding her in that cave." He replied brightly.

"Scandal?" Jerard quizzed.

"Well that proves that Richard Taylor couldn't have done it." He went on.

"It does?"

"Of course," Mrs. Winters agreed, "Richard was claustrophobic. There's no way he could have gone in the cave."

SUNDAY

THE REST OF the house was probably still sleeping when Jerard and I were making our way out on to the cliffs. I knew the first glance at Jerard that something was wrong. He was rubbing his temples and cringing like the first time he'd taken me there.

"Fiona's here." I suddenly realized that I could feel her presence with us.

"Grandpa too."

"Your grandfather hated this place, he wouldn't come here in life, let alone in death." We were surprised to find that the voice belonged to Charlie.

"Why not?" I watched him make his way over the rocks with the ease of a teenager.

"His subconscious knew that he let the love of his life die here. He used to hate coming here. I must admit sometimes I drug him out here to torture him a little. He could never understand why." Charlie said wistfully.

"He didn't mean to kill her." Jerard retorted.

"Who said he killed her? I said he let her die." Charlie was getting closer to us. "Your grandfather was weak fool. Hiding behind that Post traumatic nonsense in his later years, he didn't leave Korea any worse off than I did."

"Who killed her then?" I noted that Jerard was edging us closer to the jagged edges of the cliffs.

"You're so unlike your aunt, at least she could put two and two together. I did, you pathetic girl, she chose James, can you imagine, she chose that weak and withering man over me! I had so much more potential than James ever had. Yet she still chose him." Charlie seemed to be talking more to himself by this point. "Either way, he didn't get her in the end. Though I didn't either, that was the one flaw in it all." Somewhere in the back of my mind I heard Fiona gasp.

"You killed her?" Jerard's voice was strained.

"You didn't expect me to let her carry on with him did you? That man was incompetent after the war, she deserved a hero. I'd rather have seen her dead than in his charge."

"My grandpa was a hero. I have his purple heart, where's yours?"

"T-that's not the point! I was a prisoner of war!" Charlie roared. "She always consoled him, was always right there with him after his episodes. Korea was no picnic for me, but she never showed me that kind of . . . consideration. She wrote me! She made me fall in love with her! It wasn't my fault that she was so stupid!"

"She didn't love you." I stated the obvious.

"She should have!" Charlie growled. "She'd be alive today if she had."

"You can't chose who you fall in love with."

"It's funny that history should repeat itself. Your aunt and yourself being killed by the same man, it's curious how fate works isn't it?" I watched in horror as Charlie pulled a revolver from his coat.

"Trust me." Jerard muttered.

For the second time I was sent careening over the edge of the Cliffs against my will into Little Dublin Lake. I opened my eyes under the chilled water, Jerard held on tight to my hand, it wouldn't register until later the two other sets of hands dragging me upwards. My head broke the surface and fear surged through every inch of me as gun shots rang in my ears. I swam as hard as I could towards shore Jerard pushing behind me. We got to our feet once we reached the shallows and tore off into the wooded area near by. I tried to stop just inside the foliage.

"Claire, baby, you have to run okay? You can't stop." Jerard desperately took my face in his hands. Another gun shot sounded from the cliffs and though I felt exhausted and my legs screamed at me I nodded as he grabbed my hand and ran deeper into the woods. I hoped he knew where I was going because I was totally lost already. After what seemed like an eternity Jerard finally allowed me to slump against a tree trunk.

"Sweetheart, are you okay?" Jerard lifted my chin to look at him.

"I'm okay, are you?" I heaved as he made me turn around completely.

"Yeah, I'm great . . ." Jerard stopped abruptly, "Oh my god, Claire!"

I twisted my head around to look at the back of my left calf. Blood was streaming steadily from a hole in my jeans. Pain immediately seared through my leg, suddenly aware that a large piece of metal was at that moment lodged in my leg. I started to cry in pain and fear. I didn't even know where we were, let alone if we were safe from Charlie.

"Claire, calm down." Aunt Ona's voice rang in my head. "Take Jerard's hand." I choked back my tears and grabbed Jerard's hand.

On the edge of the cliffs Charlie shot at Jerard and I as we tried to swim to safety. In the water Jerard, Aunt Ona and James helped me to the surface. Jerard and Aunt Ona continued to help me to shore, but James, James floated to greet his old friend.

"You were my friend." He said to Charlie. "How could you betray me? How could you betray her?"

"You're not real. I'm seeing things." Charlie tried to back away from the edge of the cliffs. He didn't get very far.

"It was you all along." behind him was another transparent figure had appeared. Charlie spun around.

"Rick! No, you're dead, you died in prison."

"I'm sorry, James. I should have believed you." Richard Taylor looked around Charlie.

"It was him." James nodded to Charlie who stood frozen between the two. "He's the one who sent the police after you."

"I know. He took both of our lives from us James." Rick nodded. "I think its only fitting that we take his from him. What do you say?"

"I agree. Goodbye Charlie. I hope hell is good to you."

The gun shot rung in my ears as Aunt Ona released us. I stared at Jerard slightly horrified. Charlie was dead, the whole twisted line of events, the whole terror and mystery had finally ended.

EPILOGUE

"EVERYONE'S STARING AT me." I muttered to Jerard as he helped me through the halls of ASH the following Thursday.

"No they're not, their staring at me." Jerard shifted my bag on his shoulder.

"Oh yeah?" I nearly caught one of my crutches on anther student's foot. "Why is that?"

"Cause I'm with the most beautiful broken girl ever and they're all jealous." He replied without missing a beat.

"Thanks." I managed to laugh as we drew closer to Mrs. Lancaster's classroom. It was the part of the day I'd been dreading since I hobbled into school that morning.

"Miss. Weston, Mr. Lane." Mrs. Lancaster stopped us just outside the door.

"Mrs. Lancaster." I swallowed. She gave us an approving nod and handed me a couple of newspaper clippings before going back into the classroom. Confused we made our way into the classroom and sat in our usual seats. All the headlines included what really happened to Fiona Kelly, James Davenport, Richard Taylor and Charlie Fiske.

Jerard and I were two of the few to attend the grave side services for Charlie. The others in mourning kept casting us furtive glances, most likely afraid we were about to create a scene. Charlie was buried across the cemetery from Fiona and James, in my opinion that wasn't nearly far enough away. We watched for a moment as they started filling the grave in, before heading slowly across the graveyard towards Mom, Landon, Aiden, Sam and Shannon who were visiting Fiona's gravesite.

"It's done." Jerard told them solemnly. "The nightmare is finally over."

"It's good to know what happened to her finally. I wish Mom and Dad could have died knowing." Mom wrapped an arm around my shoulders and heaved a sigh.

I nodded as I gazed at the headstone Mom had chosen for her. Two interlocked hearts were engraved over the writing.

HERE LIES
FIONA MARY KELLY
MARCH 17, 1933 – SEPTEMBER 10, 1951

AT PEACE WITH GOD, LOVED BY ALL, AND READY AT THE SAVIORS CALL.

YE ALSO BE READY.

I nodded, looking just beyond the headstone. Fiona stood there a pleasant smile playing at her mouth, James was holding her hand at her side. Trying not to alert mom, I tapped Jerard lightly and nodded towards them. I watched Jerard's eyes grow to the size of saucers and I knew that he had seen his grandpa for the first time in ghost form. I smiled at them and suddenly remembered what Fiona had told me.

"Mom, she doesn't blame you for the dress." I told her, Mom looked at me, a shocked expression splashed across her face.

"What does that mean?" Sam stared between us.

"When I was a little girl, and Fiona was getting married she modeled her wedding dress for us. I was young at the time, running around with juice. I tripped over my own feet and tipped the whole glass over her train. She was so furious, she wouldn't speak to me for days, but how could you know that?" Mom's eyes glistened with unshed tears. I glanced at Fiona and shrugged.

"Come on, let's go home." Landon nodded towards the cars, mom nodded and led the way to the cars.

"Claire, can I have a word?" Landon requested. I nodded, and Jerard promised to meet me at the car.

"Jerard spoke with me while you were in the hospital. He said you mentioned wanting to become a Hart." Landon jumped right into it. I stared after Jerard, "Well, I know that's a huge step for you. I'd never make you make that sort of decision."

"Your mom and I are looking into the paperwork, all we need is your approval to go ahead with them." Landon informed me before I could really get going.

"I definitely approve." I grinned at him.

"Glad to hear it!" Landon gave me a one armed hug. He looked towards the cars and focused on Jerard.

"Now, about Jer . . ."

"Landon!" I groaned.

"Okay, okay," He grinned at me as we headed towards Jerard, "We'll save that rant for after the paperwork is finalized."

APPENDIX

Local Hero Returns from War
by: Eugene Haller

Corporal James Davenport returned to Alden's Hollow yesterday as a result of wounds received in the police action in Korea. Corporal Davenport was met off the train by girlfriend, Fiona Kelly and his family, after spending two weeks at Walter Reed Army Medical Center recovering from a chest wound.

Davenport Receives Special Award from Mayor
by: Rex Greenstone

Corporal James Davenport received a special award at Friday night's open of the Harvest Festival. Mayor Frederick Lake awarded him a certificate of achievement for his role in the Korean Conflict. Davenport stated modestly, "All I did was get out of there with my butt in one piece." Mayor Lake also awarded him the title of Grand Marshall of this years festivities. Coming soon, a one on one interview with Corporal Davenport about his tour in Korea.

Local Girl goes Missing
By: Ernie Bishop

After several days of searching, police officials are still on the look out for lost teen, Fiona Kelly. Kelly was reported missing on Wednesday night when she failed to return home after a trip to Alden City Park the night before. Boyfriend, war hero, James Davenport is considered a suspect in her disappearance.

Decades Old Mystery Solved

Saturday morning the body of Fiona Mary Kelly was located in a cave near Little Dublin Lake. Fifty-seven years ago Fiona Mary Kelly never returned from an outing with then boyfriend, James Davenport and friend, Charlie Fiske. Though an extensive, for the time, search ensued no one could locate the missing teen. According to reports, Kelly, Davenport and Fiske had gone to "The Cliffs" lining Little Dublin Lake to enjoy an afternoon of swimming and cliff jumping. Sources close to Kelly always maintained that she was not a good swimmer, officials say it is likely that Kelly drown and was moved to the cave after death and there was no signs of other causes of death. A memorial service for Kelly will be held near Little Dublin Lake Saturday afternoon. Anyone who knew Fiona is welcome to come share their stories and love for this lost soul finally brought to rest.

Fiona: Found at Last
By: Jerard Lane and Claire Weston

Everyone thinks of Alden's Hollow as a new age Sleepy Hollow. The small town where everyone knows everyone else, where you don't have to lock your doors at night, and where kids could stay out until after dark and parents never feared for them. Well, even Sleepy Hollow had a sinister side.

Fiona Mary Kelly was the oldest of seven children born to Henry and Elizabeth Kelly. She was close to all of her siblings during her short life, often times serving as surrogate mother to the younger ones when both of her parents needed to work to keep the family going. She wanted two things out of life, to become a nurse and to marry her high school sweetheart.

James Davenport was the middle son of Martin and Ava Davenport. He was drafted into the military and served in the Korean war at the tail end of 1950, serving in the Army and receiving several awards, medals and citations for his bravery.

James and Fiona planned to get married the summer after he got home from Korea, but Fiona didn't want to wait until the following summer so they opted for a fall wedding. So October 6, 1951 became the day that they would be come husband and wife, but they never made it to that day. Well that is to say Fiona didn't.

On September 10, 1951 Fiona went to The Cliffs with James and James' friend and Army buddy, Charlie Fiske. Charlie and James had served loyally together in trenches, and Charlie felt compelled to move to Alden's Hollow to be closer to his friend. Or so everyone thought.

The real story is James had suggested Fiona write to Charlie while in the trenches, knowing Charlie had no sweetheart of his own. In the pages Fiona extended the same care towards Charlie as she did James. That is to say that she talked about things she knew were close to him, his car, his family and faithful Lab at home, Bebe. In those seemingly innocent pages Charlie fell in love with Fiona.

That's where the sappy love story turns vicious. James returned to the States with a chest wound and Charlie was captured by the enemy. They lost contact for years, until Charlie showed up in Alden's Hollow just a month before the wedding. Needless to say, Charlie was shocked that Fiona was still willing to marry James after his nightmares, hallucinations, and every day fears such as a car back firing. Charlie saw him as weak, half a man, not worthy of Fiona's ever lasting love.

On September 10, 1951 Fiona, Charlie and James went cliff jumping at The Cliffs. Fiona was a horrible swimmer, but both boys were great so they figured she'd be safe. No one knew she was actually putting herself in the most danger ever. Charlie was determined to have her, and if he couldn't no one could. No one knows if Charlie could predict his black outs or if Charlie simply took the opportunity he was given, but while James paced in the water believing he was on guard duty, Charlie drown Fiona in Little Dublin Lake.

Richard Taylor, another military man, was eventually accused and convicted of the crime. Charlie – whom people thought of as a hero – gave a tip to a local policemen and they promptly acted upon it. Richard Taylor died in prison, leaving behind a wife and daughter, who never thought he was guilty.

James never knew he let his fiancé die, he never knew what had become of her period. He died living a full life but never fully forgetting his true love that he lost so unexpectedly. Charlie committed suicide after he heard voices in his head – the ghosts of his past finally catching up with him, and Fiona. Fiona was left to decay in a cave in the woods near Little Dublin lake. We discovered her remains just prior to this assignment being due. She had a proper burial – something that was long over due. All families involved finally found the closure they were looking for decades later.

Obituary: Charles Henry Fiske

Charles "Charlie" Fiske of Alden's Hollow passed away Sunday morning at the age of seventy-nine.

Charlie was born in Boston, Massachusetts on April 19, 1929 where he attended local public schools before being drafted into the Korean War in 1951. He served faithfully in the United States Army becoming a prisoner of war. At the time Charlie had been a robust man of nearly two hundred pounds, when he was returned to the care of the Americans, Charlie barely weighed a hundred pounds and suffered greatly at the hands of the enemy. He was welcomed home to Boston with a hero's welcome.

Charlie moved to Alden's Hollow six months after returning to the States to find a friend, James Davenport who had become very dear to him.

Charlie worked for many years as a staff writer for the Alden Daily Bugle.

He was preceded in death by his parents, George and Linda Fiske, and several Aunts and Uncles.

He is survived by brother Donald Fiske of Portland, Oregon and sister Peggy McMaster of Ft. Worth, Texas as well as five nieces and nephews.

Charlie was a good man who will live on in the hearts of those who loved him. May he now rest in peace.

Obituary: Fiona Kelly

After decades on uncertainty the family of Fiona Kelly are laying her to rest.

Fiona Mary Kelly was born on March 17, 1933 to Michael and Elizabeth Kelly. She was the oldest of seven children.

Fiona lived a short but meaningful life. Though she was sickly in her earlier years, Fiona wanted nothing more than to become a nurse. She was an uncommonly kind soul that just wanted to make a difference in the lives of those around her.

Fiona was preceded in death by her grandparents; William and Anne Kelly, and Tully and Murron MacAndrews.

She was survived by her brothers; Henry (Martha) Kelly of Indianapolis, IN, and Liam (Gena) Kelly of West Branch, MI. Sisters; Eleanor (Daniel) Martin of Allendale, MI, Christine (Hank) O'Dell of Joliet, IL, Adele (Terry) Esson of Green Bay, WI. And Amelia (Landon) Hart of Alden's Hollow, MI. As well as several cousins, nieces, nephews.

The Kelly family would like to thank everyone for respecting their privacy during this difficult time.

Obituary: James E. Davenport

James Edward Davenport of Alden's Hollow passed Sunday morning after several years battling lung cancer. He was surrounded by loving family members.

James was born to January 14, 1932 to Martin and Ava Davenport. The middle child of three.

James attended Alden Senior High before being drafted into the Korean War. He served for nearly a year when he suffered a chest wound and was sent home.

In 1965 James married his wife, Sharon and had three children.

He worked for the majority of his life at the courthouse as a maintenance man and was often giving the task of winding the clock in the tower.

James was preceded in death by his parents and brother Eugene Davenport.

He is survived by his wife Sharon Davenport of Alden's Hollow, Sons; Dean Davenport of Watertown, New York, and Timothy (Amber) Davenport of Denver, CO. and daughter, Amanda (Jeremy) Lane of Alden's Hollow.

Funeral arrangements are being handled by Bixby Funeral home.

Made in the USA
Monee, IL
29 October 2022